OVERCOMING
A TWO-FACED
PASTOR

Other Works By Author

Orphaned, Fostered and Adopted
Collection of 89 Poems Volume 1
Collection of 89 Poems Volume 2
Collection of 89 Poems Volume 3
Collection of 89 Poems Volume 4
Overcoming a Two-Faced Pastor
Collection of 89 Poems Volume 5
Collection of 89 Poems Volume 6
Collection of 89 Poems Volume 7

OVERCOMING
A TWO-FACED
PASTOR

by

Marissa Kline-Gonzales

But they that wait upon the LORD shall renew their strength; they shall mount up with wings as eagles; they shall run, and not be weary; and they shall walk, and not faint. Isaiah 40:31 (KJV)

Praise for Overcoming A Two-Faced Pastor

"Many go through this situation and cannot speak of them. It is nice to have a book that shares it, but that points people to our Lord and Saviour."
Gina F. Missionary to Zambia, Africa

"As a whole, this book is a must-read book exposing what is evil and defining a genuine Christian faith."
Pastor Cesar

Dedications

This book is for non-Christians and Christians,
man or woman, young and old.

Her Upbringing

Amy: *You never asked me if it was okay to see me alone.*
Pastor: *Well, you didn't have a husband.*

Did you get a massage from him?
No, I would never let him touch me!

Make sure she signs a contract, so she won't tell anyone about this.

I could have taken you to court.

She has a relational problem.

You could have lost your job.

You should apologize to Pastor!

She'll never be happy!

These words continuously whirled in her head every night. Somehow, she could not get over what had happened at the second meeting and could not understand what she did wrong. They called themselves Christians and this is how they treated her?

Amy Stiles was a shy and simple girl. Born in Manila, Philippines where at that time, the majority of the people were Catholics and less than 5% were from Protestant Christian denominations. Her family was once one of the die-hard Catholics that lived in the Philippines, but by the time she was born her family had converted to born-again Christianity.

Amy grew up singing children's Bible songs in church with other children, memorizing verses, hearing Bible stories, reading the Bible not only in church but also at home, and having fond memories of her family going to church instead of the traditional sit down, listen and kneel to pray.

God and her family helped instill in Amy a child-like faith that grew so strong that as a young girl she already believed in an Almighty God who controls everything in her life, like the typhoon, her family's poverty situation and life itself. She knew there was a greater person higher than us and that is Jesus Christ. She learned as a young girl that things like clothes, money and life could be taken away at any time, but as long as we still have our faith, it didn't matter. As the

Bible says, *Hath not God chosen the poor of this world rich in faith, and heirs of the kingdom which he hath promised to them that love him? James 2:5.* This verse rang true in her heart.

Tragically, her birth mother died when she was seven years old. She experienced a total of two orphanages and two foster homes in her lifetime. As a young child she had been through a lot; Missing her birth family that she grew to love, being mistreated by foster families and care takers in the orphanage and longing for a new family to love her. Despite the many tears she shed at night behind closed doors her child-like faith was unshakeable. She may have had many tribulations and trials while growing up, but she knew that her God was going to turn it around and bless her like Job and Joseph in the Bible. It was just a matter of time. While lying in bed at night back in the orphanage days she would always look at the moon. It was a reminder to her that just like God, He is always watching and caring for her.

Miraculously at age nine, Amy was adopted to an American couple. Her dream of having a family came true. God opened this path so that she could help her family in the Philippines. Her faith in God was so strong that through good times and bad she remained firm, trusting in God alone. Amy realized that her faith is definitely a gift from God and no one can take that away.

When she was adopted in the U.S., she had parents that prioritized church. They went to church every Sunday morning and evening and also every

Wednesday for prayer meeting. If there was a revival, they would attend church the whole week. It was a must and arguing about it was not an option.

By her adolescent years, Amy was part of the Teens for Christ group doing different activities with other teenagers. On Saturdays, Track Distribution and Visitation day, she knocked on people's doors and invited them to come to church. She did this from seventh grade all the way up to her senior year.

Every summer, the church teenagers went to a Christian camp for a whole week. One of the church camps they traveled to was The Wilds in North Carolina. They not only had a lot of fun times there and activities galore for the young people, but they also taught teenagers to make a lifetime commitment to God and to be faithful in reading His Word. This was where Amy accepted Christ as her Savior. Some people may call it brain-washing, but Amy knew deep down that there is a loving God in heaven who deserves our worship.

She also helped out in the Bus Ministry every Sunday, which involved picking up kids from the cities and countryside and bringing them to church. Amy's church picked up over 100 children and adults and faithfully brought them to church every Sunday. Money was not an object, because the pastors along with the many volunteers in that church were more concerned about the souls of the people than the expense of the Sunday bus routine. Amy loved those humble people so much and knew that ministering with them was part of her calling.

Amy and her sister attended Christian School most of their lives where dress code was not an option but a requirement. They were required to wear dresses or skirts below their knees to school; Nothing could be see-through, tight, or skimpy, and no shirts could be low enough to show cleavage or skirts too short. Modesty played a big role in their Christian living.

Every Thursday was chapel time in school where they had either a missionary preach or pastors stop by. By 11th grade, Amy had dedicated her life to Christ to use her to do whatever He called her to do. By the time she had graduated high school she had already made a commitment to God to keep herself pure and wait for the man God had planned for her to marry (a commitment she kept and never regretted).

However, being raised in a Christian home all her life had created an inner conflict deep down in Amy's heart. She wanted something new. She began to grow a deep detachment from the routine and methodical Christian life. Somehow, Amy wanted more than just what she saw, but since she didn't want to disrespect her parents she went with the flow hoping one day she could get out of it.

After high school, Amy followed the suggestion of one of her high school teachers and attended Word of Life Bible Institute in Florida. Amy's heart was tender toward missions, and although she had a compassion for and a desire to help the orphans and poor, she was unsure how to go about it. She was young and still searching for her true identity.

While at the Bible Institute, Amy and her classmates scrutinized several books of the Bible and were expected to have Quiet Time devotions every morning and every night. She took her classes very seriously and didn't get into any trouble. The only punishment she ever received was for petty things like leaving her shoes outside or forgetting to do little chores. Other than that, she was focused on all her subjects and pleased God with all her heart. Before the year ended, it was a requirement to read the entire Bible and involve herself in Summer Missions in order to pass. If Amy wasn't familiar with the Bible growing up, she was now definitely indoctrinated in the scriptures.

Away From Home

A FTER GRADUATION, AMY Stiles incredibly found a job as a flight attendant, an influence from her aunt who used to be a flight attendant for Eastern Airline. She wanted to see the world and the closest airport based near home was John F. Kennedy Airport.

At the age of 20, God allowed her to see the good and bad side of what the real world was all about through this job. It was a real eye opener.

The good part was that she traveled around the world, made new friends of different nationalities, worked and saved her own money, and lived independently on her own. But the negative side was that it all was completely opposite from the way she was raised. She was raised in a strict school, in an overprotective home, and a conscientious church.

In this life, she saw many young adults wasting their lives by going clubbing, bar hopping, spending so much money on booze, and becoming addicted to alcohol and smoking. They were like college students partying every night. And some struggled with pornography.

Amy also heard profane words, noticed swearing and the frequent use of God's name in vain—a vast difference from what she knew growing up in Lancaster, Pennsylvania. She learned to ignore most of that. Besides, swearing was never a part of her character.

There was lusting, flirting, cheating and sleeping around. Many of Amy's co-workers were already on their second or third marriages. Working in the airline can be glamorous if you live near your family. If not, those four, three or two-day trips can be a lonely life. Amy soon realized that she was surrounded by "men lovers of their own selves." Much more, they looked at life without any godly purpose or morals. She knew she had to guard her heart for *"...the devil as a roaring lion, walketh about, seeking whom he may devour. I Peter 5:8*

At first the airline placed the new flight attendants in hotels for approximately two days. Then after that they had to find a place on their own. By word of mouth, she and other flight attendants transferred to another place similar to a dormitory. The 11th floor was known as the Party Floor, although they didn't know until later. When the elevator door opened, the cigarette smell smacked you right in the face. You saw some of them sitting in the hallway smoking and drinking with music blaring. There were three bunk beds in the room and supposedly 10 or so people living there but since everyone was mostly traveling, going in and out, you took whatever bed was available. It worked most of the time. The airline term they called their home away from home was, "Crash pad", a place for them to sleep and work again the next day. It was a way to save money while living in an expensive city. While many of them were away from home for the first time, they were just thankful to find a place where they could reside. They were literally left on their own. She lived there for six months and eventually moved to another crash pad in Queens, New York. This crash pad was calmer and quieter. Eight ladies resided in this bedroom while they shared the living room with other people next door.

Amy noticed that when some of her co-workers had problems they had no one to look to for hope, peace and happiness. In her own life God was her purpose, including her hope, peace and happiness. She saw the people around her as people needing Christ in their lives but who were blinded by the world. Not wanting to end up like them, she realized she needed to get back to church soon. Plus, she also faced a lot of sexual harassment from work. After all she was only 20 years old, young, naïve and innocent. She never had a boyfriend until she was in her mid-20s. She also never heard of Sex Trade or Human Trafficking until she was in her mid-30s. but she was thankful God protected her from all that. She thought for sure that church would be a place of refuge, safety and away from troubles, a place where she can get away from the worldly things.

S OON AFTER, AMY found an Asian church in the Yellow Book that had similar beliefs as her old church. It was called Victory United Church. The great thing about living on the East Coast is that you can choose which nationality of church to attend; Polish, Korean, Chinese, African and Filipino Churches, to name some. Amy was so thrilled to have that option because she had always wanted to reconnect with her Filipino roots. She was somewhat unsure, since she had forgotten some of her native traditions and, worse yet, how to speak her original language, and yet she was hopeful. Even though she was raised American from nine years old and up, Amy decided as long as the gospel was preached that was a start. She called the church hoping for a van or bus to pick her up. Later on, she realized this church didn't really have a van ministry.

As Amy began attending, she talked mostly to the pastor; After all, if anyone should be trusted, it should be the pastor. He was one of the first people to pick Amy up; However, he was always alone. Amy couldn't understand how a pastor who knew a lot of people would pick-up people by himself, but she made herself think that it must be okay since he was the pastor. Consequently, she put a barrier between him and herself because she didn't think what he did was right.

Some people in that church considered the pastor a father figure, especially those whose father was deceased or was far away. Others looked up to him as a top leader with high regard, without flaws, or as someone filled with the Holy Spirit, someone whom no one can disrespect. But Amy viewed him as someone to watch out for with great discernment. There was something about him she did not trust.

Amy was eager to be close to the church people. However, since she was unable to frequently attend church she was unable to get close to them yet or even ask for their phone numbers. So, she called the number from the Yellow Book which was connected to the pastor. He took her to places like fine restaurants, New York City and other places. But in the end, Amy felt guilty because she knew he was married and had two kids. Amy was concerned that if someone saw her alone with the pastor, they would be in big trouble. She was sure someone would feel offended. In spite of this, when she was alone with the pastor, he had a way of making her feel special; How flattering to think that this man of God who had a busy schedule had set aside his precious time to spend it with her.

The first Bible Study he ever took her to was at a church member's house. He picked her up at her crash pad. When they went in she quietly observed as people slowly arrived. She felt very much at home. She had a lot of things in common with the people: her looks, her skin color, a friendly demeanor. Then Pastor Janus put money on the table for food. So, her first impression of Bible study was that you paid for the food. She remembered giving $5.00 so she could eat. But that wasn't really necessary. After years of going there, she never saw anyone give money. Bible Study was voluntary. An individual or a family could volunteer their time, home and refreshments for the Lord, so they might continue to fellowship with other believers. It was the first and last time she ever saw him do it. But then again, who questioned the pastor's motives? Then she noticed he would religiously take food home. Now he had a free meal for tomorrow.

THIS CHURCH KEPT a lot of their Filipino traditions; For instance, someone's elders were respectfully called Tita (Auntie) or Tito (Uncle). And the eldest were referred to as Lola (Grandma) or Lolo (Grandpa). Not one person called each other Mr. or Mrs. In that sense the church had unity. It also had unity as its members believed they were brothers and sisters in Christ.

After each church service they had a luncheon with Filipino food, and Amy really enjoyed tasting Filipino food all over again (something she missed, growing up in Pennsylvania). Overall, the church was still considered a Filipino-American church with an English-speaking pastor.

She had a deep hunger to be with church people, hoping that this church provided that. She was still on call at work and weekends weren't always available to go to church. She did have a tiny group of Christian friends at work, but Amy hardly saw them due to their busy schedules. One of her first hangouts with this pastor was in her first year at the Airline. This pastor took advantage of her loneliness and away from home feeling. After he took her out for lunch, he asked her if she wanted to go to his house. Amy was more than ready to take a break from her chaotic crash pad life so when he offered she thought lightly of it. He drove her to his home and his wife happened to be coming back from work. She was glad that she was there, but she noticed she was more interested in watching TV than socializing or making her feel comfortable. She did greet her but very quickly. Later that same day, the two-faced pastor showed her a gun that he possessed telling her that he used to be a police officer. Then he carefully put back the gun in the protective case. Again, she didn't really know what was his purpose in that situation but went on with life.

Amy was young, naïve, and in her early 20s. Since she was alone in a big city, she stayed in that church and tried her very best to attend every Sunday service, Wednesday Prayer Meeting and Bible Study on Friday despite her hectic schedule. Eventually, she even participated in the choir where she noticed there were many talented singers in that church. Amazed at how they could sing Amy took singing lessons from the choir director. One day when Pastor Janus was driving Amy, she mentioned to him that she was taking singing lessons. He said to her, "To sing properly you must use your diaphragm" and then he put his hand on her mid-section, to show where the diaphragm was. Amy was stunned. She thought to herself, *Why couldn't he illustrate it on himself instead of touching me?* But to this man it seemed normal to do that. Was he trying to see how far he could go?

One time, while alone in his van, the pastor asked Amy for money. He said someone died in the Philippines and they needed help for the funeral. Amy told him when her birth mother died they just put her in a cheap coffin since they were so poor. He nonchalantly showed Amy a load of cash that he had collected from different people, flipping through the thick wad of $20 bills like pages in his hands. So, he talked Amy into giving him some cash, but she never heard the result of the funeral. Looking back, it is now clear that what he did was wrong. All fundraising or charity work should be done from the pulpit, not in private. But was he doing this on purpose? And how many more people had he done this to?

There was one time when the pastor told the congregation from the pulpit that he promised his children long ago – before coming to America – a trip to Disney World. Then he asked the church to financially help him. This caught Amy by surprise. She knew her pastor in Pennsylvania would never ask the church for this kind of favor. As a matter of fact, she knew no pastor would be bold enough to put such a burden on their congregation. Now people had the dilemma of whether they should help or not. On the one hand, they didn't want to be greedy and should just help him and his family out, but on the other hand, some felt he used the church to get what he wanted instead of working hard for it. However, due to pressure, Amy was one of the people that gave him money that day, so they could fulfill their fantasy. It was definitely one of those events that stuck out in Amy's mind.

Another unforgettable time, also alone in his van, the pastor explained to Amy that he gave massages to people and implied that she should try it too. Amy was completely flabbergasted and could not believe what she heard. She was conservatively raised and taught that it was wrong to let anyone other than your spouse touch you, because temptation was so great on both sides. Amy saw this as a time bomb waiting to go off.

Amy thought for sure deep in her heart that pastors were supposed to stay holy, blameless and not do things that would cause people to talk. Yet her pastor told her that he had other customers. After hearing these things, she became discouraged. She knew that her pastor in Pennsylvania would never do such a thing. So, she decided to take a break from church because of the many warning signs.

Many people in that church were also suspicious of what the pastor did with these young ladies alone in his van, taking them to places. However, it wasn't something anyone could really put their finger on and say for sure. Instead, the response was often, "I shouldn't be thinking this way. I shouldn't be having these kinds of thoughts. These are wrong thoughts. Leaders wouldn't do those things." Unfortunately, those thoughts kept people silent. People were afraid to come forward.

Amy was very discouraged and shocked that a church like this could even exist. She figured since the pastor was not any different from the world, why go to church? So, she left the church for quite a while—more than several months.

D URING THIS TIME away from church she was left confused and bewildered, wondering why the church let their pastor do these things. No one seemed to do anything about it. So, she figured it must be ok. Amy tried to live like him, since he had done those things for many, many years. It was then that Amy started traveling to places with someone of an opposite sex (but no intimacy happened), dating unsaved guys (but nothing serious), and hanging out with friends at bars (but she never drank). These were things that she would normally not do; She knew her limits. Even so, Amy believed if the pastor had acted biblically, she would have never done these things or followed his example. Instead, she would have walked a godly, Christ-like path. And she wondered, *How many more people has the pastor caused to stumble?*

The Bible says, "*A disciple is not greater than his teacher, but everyone when fully trained will be like his teacher. Luke 6:40.*" Amy knew people can never be biblical leaders and truly mature until they realize that God has called them to live as examples to others. They must model spiritual virtues and influence others in positive ways. Without biblical and godly models, we can be cast into a restless sea that is tossed to and fro.

ONE DAY AMY'S co-workers who did not go to church were looking for massagers. When she told them that her pastor gave massages (thinking she was helping them) they started laughing at her and making jokes. Humiliated, she thought to herself, "If the unsaved think it's wrong for a pastor to massage, how much more for us Christians?"

About this time, one of Amy's roommates worked as a bartender in addition to working for the airline. Amy was tempted to work at a bar too to make extra money because she had a lot of responsibility. Before, the decision would have been black or white and a yes or no answer. After attending that Asian church, she saw it as a grey area. She was single and earning one income for the many people she supported, including her biological family in the Philippines. Amy figured since her pastor made extra income through massaging, she didn't see why she couldn't do the same. The main difference was that the pastor lived for free and had free utilities, plus his wife was a nurse. The temptation to earn money working in a bar was very great and enticing, but then Amy looked at what the Bible had to say: For the love of money is the root of all evil. I Timothy 6:10 But my God shall supply all of my needs. Philippians 4:19

In addition, Amy asked herself, "What would Jesus do?" She knew being a devoted Christian and working at a bar did not mix. She wanted to set an example to the people around her, showing that her heart, time and life were purely for Christ. Convicted by His Word, Amy dismissed the idea of working in a bar. Without even consciously trying, she stands out because she doesn't belong to the world. She has been chosen to belong to God.

PEOPLE THAT KNEW Amy from work knew her as a girl that never swore, said God's name in vain, or used other profanity. They knew she didn't smoke, drink beer or wine and never dared try drugs. She knew also that flirting was a dangerous thing. She was committed to saving herself for her future husband. No matter how hard people tried to change her life or influence her in a bad way, her fear in God was so strong. She knew that her Omnipotent God had power to send people to hell or to heaven. At the same time, deep in her heart she loved Jesus Christ so much that she wanted to please Him more than anyone or anything in this world.

Even though Amy was young and had a good job, her future looked bleak to her. She knew if she continued to live and hang out with the worldly crowd, her life would eventually turn upside down. She would disappoint her parents and those that loved her. Amy is thankful that God grasped her heart before she went too far.

Several months later, Amy did return to church, since she saw it as her only escape to get away from the things of this world. The people of the church had missed her and welcomed her back with great enthusiasm. God's love was definitely evident in the people that went there, and this was why Amy returned. When one church member died, everyone grieved with pain. Their pain became everyone's pain; Their loss became everyone's loss. It was as if the church was united through good times and bad. The church members became the church family that Amy had always dreamed of.

By this time, Amy was already living just walking distance from the church. The living conditions were much better than her first crash pad. Overall, calling for a ride was no longer needed. She started to hang around other families from that church that truly were saints and who dearly loved God. From them she was able to see and copy how Christian individuals and families were supposed to act, have fun and live. She knew the way the pastor was living was not the way. She also knew living in a strict religious environment was not the way either. There had to be a balance in a Christian living. She knew deep down there was a difference between having a relationship with Christ and having a religion. Amy's time with them had helped to shape her; She had become confident in her faith by sharing that love with other people.

THROUGHOUT THOSE YEARS, however, Amy heard of long-time members leaving Victory United, one a devoted Christian family of six. They led worship service, managed the children's choir, taught Sunday School, were active in Vacation Bible School, participated in Medical Missions and joined the adult choir. They had attended that church for over 17 years. They left in 2003, because the pastor had a way of twisting words around with people, lying, gossiping and making others look bad. When they left, the mother was so hurt that to this day she still sees stained tear drops on her Bible. Not once did the pastor try to mend the problem.

Amy was sad to see them go because she had learned to love many of these people as her brothers and sisters in Christ, but then she also didn't want to get involved.

She had grown accustomed to the many people that were still attending, so she continued to attend despite what she was hearing. She wondered, though, how many more families had left before she even came to this church. These thoughts put a red flag in her mind. She knew something was not being done right.

Some may wonder why she didn't just leave or switch to a different church since she experienced so many bad things already. There were many reasons. One reason was because she had learned to love and trust the people in that church—not necessarily the pastor, but the people themselves. Because she was away from home, Amy felt she needed to have a connection like that in her life. She needed someone to turn to for Christian guidance. A second reason was that she was giving the pastor the benefit of the doubt. Since the Bible talks about forgiveness, being merciful and loving and most of all grace, she stayed hoping that one day he would change. But instead he got worse and worse.

ONE DAY A church friend and Amy went clothes shopping and Amy asked her friend, "Do you sometimes feel there's like a competition in the way people dress in our church?" She grew up in that church all her life and could not see any difference. However, in Amy's opinion, modesty was not preached as it should. She could understand the young people dressing immodestly but did not agree when church leaders like Sunday School teachers and a deacon's wife dressed in a worldly way, with blouses so low, dresses so short and clothes so tight that no one would ever guess that they were part of a church.

One of the men confronted the pastor about the way some of the ladies dressed (e.g. see-through and tight clothes). The pastor responded to him, "What can I do about it?" Eventually, he did leave the church along with his wife.

Another family of four also left. They had been members for over 17 years when they decided to leave the church. The husband was a deacon, Sunday School Superintendent and a Sunday School teacher for many years. They were a highly respected Christian family and were very loved by everyone.

They left the church because they disagreed with the leadership structure of the church. The husband repeatedly told the pastor and the board that the biblical way is to have a plurality of leaders. They paid lip service to him for many years, but nothing was done. He suggested to them that, instead of only one pastor as the leader, which often can lead to dictatorship, there should be several leaders just like in the Bible. For example, there were 12 apostles with equal authority; Not one was above the other. That way, there is a check and balance in the leadership. He warned them that there would be a problem in the church if no one was allowed to question the pastor or if he was the only authority in the church. But the deacons all turned a blind eye on his concern.

Soon people that left the church began to have a slow rippling effect. A member of 20 plus years eventually left in 2006 because the pastor destroyed their reputation during gossip time at Bible Study. The father was a chairman of the board of deacons and a Sunday School teacher for singles and professionals. His children all grew up in the church.

Regarding the pastor he said, "He would present himself as a lowly, humble, pitiful servant who would purportedly go out of his way to help the poor and needy just to solicit their sympathy and exploiting on their sentimentalism. They would even pour their last penny not knowing it support his vices. To those who had awareness to discern his manipulative ways in controlling the church and those who have awoken from their slumber brought about by his charismatic innuendos, he presents himself as a fierce, devouring beast ready to swallow you to shame and use Bible Study fellowships to rumor monger and destroy your integrity... and finally excommunicate you from 'his' church domain to avoid exposing his true ways to others."

He broke down his obsession into three parts: travels, money and young girls. Sometimes he got it all in one sweep, like when he was able to manipulate the board of deacons into giving him one-year sabbatical leave with pay and a free round-trip ticket to the Philippines. A member even allowed him to use her condo in Bonifacio Global City, a community for the elites. He went by himself while his wife and children stayed in the U.S.

Stories like this made you questions his ethics and morals but no one seemed brave enough to confront him. If someone was, Amy never heard the results. Most people just left.

AMY NOTICED A sex video in the home of one of the former deacons. He was Amy's friend; One she would have never thought was ever addicted to anything like that. He was humble and meek and worked quietly in that church for many years. But when Amy saw the sex video, she confronted him about it and he told her it was his brother's. Although Amy felt this was a bit suspicious (since he was living alone) she still informed the pastor because she knew it was wrong and was not a good example as a deacon.

Amy privately told the pastor outside the building where no one could see or hear because the deacon was a dear friend. Her intention was not to get him in trouble or dismissed from his position, but to encourage counseling or something like that. The pastor's response was shocking and left Amy dumbfounded. He said, "What do you expect, he is a man!" It totally left her troubled and sense of morality confused.

Years later, a churchgoer told her that he too confronted the deacons about one of their deacons buying sex videos in a store. Instead of saying, "Well, we will talk to him, verify things first and if it is true maybe we can counsel him and help him through this addiction," they merely attacked the church goer with many questions such as, "How do you know it was sex videos?" "Do you go to this store often?" Feeling discouraged, the church goer never brought it up again and eventually left the church. The meeting was definitely not handled in the biblical way.

One summer, Amy went to New York City with a guy friend when the temperature happened to be extremely hot over 100 degrees. Humidity was high causing people to sweat more than usual. Then around the corner as she just recently got off the train a man put his hand over her eyes and covered half of her face. She said to herself out of annoyance, I better know this person really well to get in my personal space. When he finally let go she was surprised to find out it was her pastor. Who's ever heard of a pastor putting their hands on one of their congregation's face? That's absurd. She tried to hide her disbelief and shock and just smiled it off to her friend. They chatted with each other for a little bit and went on their own way although she felt appalled that a pastor would do such a thing.

ONCE AMY HAD more days off from work she volunteered to help out in a Sunday School class. She gave 100% of her time and effort to be there every Sunday and to prepare for every lesson too, just in case the teacher was absent. She did it all for the Lord. Later on, that same teacher passed the responsibility to Amy, since she was busy with nursing school. Even though Amy was still not a member of the church she gladly accepted her offer to teach. To her she'd rather see the children learn about Jesus than them running around in the fellowship hall.

Amy taught 3rd and 4th grade Sunday School for about 10 years. She loved watching the children grow and become teenagers. She had a program called Bible Olympics where the kids competed with each other with things like who could say the most verses, who brought the most visitors, who brought their Bible and had a perfect attendance. At the end of every six months, Amy had an award party for them. She bought them prizes and candies with her own money, but it was all for the Lord. One child said, "It was like Christmas again."

Marriage

I N 2004, PASTOR JANUS'S godson, a handsome, quiet man named Mark, happened to move into the parsonage. He was about four years older than Amy Stiles, and it seemed that they were encouraged to be together. Amy, however, wasn't really sure if she should meddle with him because, after all, he didn't really have a job. Even though he went to college and had two degrees, he seemed to lack ambition. He cleaned the church for $800 dollars a month when he had a degree in Physics and Bible Exposition under his belt. But to Amy something about him just did not add up right. Some people even called him "Pastor" since he hung out with all the other pastors. Later in life she finally understood that he did have a degree in Physics but for Bible Exposition he had one semester left to get his degree.

At the same time Amy tried to start a Young Singles Fellowship group. She noticed the need for young singles to fellowship, but the church did not have the ministry. There were several singles but most of them were very shy and introverted. So, the godson, also single, and Amy were together a lot along with a few other young singles trying to get the ministry going. It seemed they needed more encouragement from the leaders, such as the deacons, to get the ministry started but that wasn't done.

The church did have a Singles ministry before, but when those people got married the ministry literally disappeared or died out and it was up to the new generation to start it again. However, without the help or encouragement of the leaders the ministry had no back bone and it would fail.

ONE OF THE oldest and longest members and former deacons of that church encouraged Amy by telling her that Mark's family owned a lot of properties in the Philippines, but she replied back, "It's not his property though, it's his family's." There's a big difference in that; Even she knew it. You had to work hard to own something if it's not just your parents passing it down to you. She was shocked by this member's comment since he'd been a member and a Christian for so long.

More than once Pastor Janus said to Amy regarding Mark, "Amy, he has a degree in Physics, so he won't have a hard time getting a good job." Words that come from a pastor's mouth are usually true and good. So, when his godson asked Amy to be his girlfriend she accepted him into her life. She dated him for several months and chose him above all the other guys that had liked her because of her pastor's encouragement. Many times, she tried to break up with him because of the way he treated her, but it was difficult. Mark was determined to keep Amy in his life. As a result, she stayed.

It was drilled into Amy at a very young age to marry a Christian man, not necessarily for money or good looks or brain but the priority was spiritual maturity. So, Amy figured, since he went to church every Sunday he must be a Christian. Plus, for a pastor to recommend him, he must be pretty good. But should pastors be in the business of match making? Amy doesn't think so, especially if the prediction doesn't come true. The spouse that marries him would end up living with him, not the pastor.

When Amy brought Mark to her parents after becoming serious, they tried to tell her that he should get a real job first and get his citizenship before they were married. Amy tried telling them that it was okay since his aunt was a doctor and most of his family was in the nursing field. She taught standing up for him was her job despite the desperate plea from her parent. She was clinging to words that her pastor had said to her. Unfortunately, Amy was very naïve regarding immigrants and visas then, since all those were taken care of for her during her adoption process in the Philippines. So Amy trusted her pastor, thinking he should know best. She was in New York most of the time and, far from home, she was getting only encouragement from Pastor Janus and some of the church people.

E NGAGEMENT WAS A little stifling. She accepted her fiancé into her life, hoping one day he would get a good job like his uncle had said. Having experienced poverty as a young girl, Amy did not want to repeat history. She remembered her brother-in-law asking her one day if it was common practice to try to match the non-citizen with the U.S. citizen. But Amy didn't know how to answer him.

Amy and the pastor's godson were friends for four months, dated for eight months and were engaged for a year. Hoping this guy was what the pastor said he was, Amy got married a month before their birthdays, at age 25. He was 29. Approximately 50 people from her New York church drove several hours to her home church in Lancaster, Pennsylvania to see them get married, yet Pastor Janus had a meeting to attend in Canada. Even though the wedding announcement had been in the church bulletin for almost a year, the pastor still planned to go somewhere else.

The people in the church and Amy were such a close-knit group that Amy had the choir director as her wedding planner, her sister was Amy's make-up artist, two men were the wedding decorators, another did the bulletin, one decorated her veil, a sweet couple were the photographers, and so much more. Plus, during their wedding a couple from her Filipino church sang a beautiful song for them, and it was very endearing.

Everything they ever needed was in that church, for God's love was shared inside and out. What would have been an extremely expensive wedding with a total of 215 attendees cost them only one fourth of the price. Amy gave credit to God and God's people in that church who, time and time again, showed her what true Christianity and true love was all about.

S ADLY THOUGH, EVEN in the very beginning of their marriage Amy noticed her husband struggling to get a good job. Since he had no experience teaching, most schools didn't want him. Surprisingly, the two-faced pastor advised them to have separate checking accounts and split their bills in half because he and his wife did it too. For example, Amy paid for the mortgage and her husband paid for the rest of the bills. It was nice at first. Amy felt very independent saving her own money. But within less than two years, her husband had depleted all of their wedding money unbeknownst to her. He was also secretly paying part of his bills with his credit card, which caused tremendous debt. Amy's worst nightmare came true.

Amy did talk to some of the leaders in the church about the advice that the pastor gave them, but they only paid lip service to her and did not really confront the pastor himself. They reiterated, "Well the Bible says ... 'the two shall be one flesh.' So, everything you have including money should be all together not separate," as if to imply that they were at fault for listening to the pastor when they were just following his advice. But the deacons were very careful not to make the pastor look bad.

It was then that Amy realized the leaders in that church had a hard time facing the Truth, as if to say bad things about the pastor was a sinful act even though what she and some other members said was true. The deacons turned a blind eye to what people said.

Another humble family of four decided to leave in 2007. They were active in Singles Ministry, Married Fellowship Ministry, Adult Choir, and the wife was once the president of Ladies Fellowship. They left the church because they were not comfortable with the pastor leading the church. They noticed there was favoritism and had detected partiality from the pastor. And, sadly, they too experienced being snubbed by the pastor himself, even though they were members for eight years.

They also noticed that this pastor had ministries outside the church (staying away for several weeks and even months) rather than spending time with the members. They said, "Because of his outside ministries he doesn't have time with his own church people."

I N 2010, ANOTHER member of 15 years with three grown children left the church. Though they liked the people and the friendships that they made, they had disagreed for years with the way leadership was done and eventually decided the preaching was not helping them grow spiritually. The man was a treasurer, a deacon and a bookkeeper. It seemed that church leadership had been a problem for years, but no one was doing anything about it.

The man had mentioned to Amy about low-powered distant culture vs. the high-powered distant culture. He said the reason why this church still exists is because of high-powered distant culture. Wikipedia explains these words this way— People in societies with a high-powered distance are more likely to conform to a hierarchy where "everybody has a place and which needs no further justification." In societies with a low-powered distance, individuals tend to try to distribute power equally. In such societies, inequalities of power among people would require additional justification.

The church has adopted this high-powered culture, even churches in the United States. Power distance was not distributed equally. People from many countries such as the Philippines looked up to this pastor almost like a king. No one was allowed to question his conduct, preaching, and personal life because of his position. But the Bible clearly talks about how this type of control can lead to a sin. It's called pride. If the church was not allowed to question the pastor, then who would? Were members just supposed to let him get away with immoral misconduct until someone got brutally hurt? Of course not! She believes she must stand up for the right now.

Many U.S. residents rarely hear about this low- and high-powered distant culture. It's difficult for many to believe that this practice still exists in a Bible believing church. It wasn't until after Amy left the church that she heard about it.

Then another young couple left the church. Since most of their close friends were leaving they decided to leave too. Plus, they also did not agree with how the leadership was being handled.

A FTER THREE YEARS, Amy and her husband had a son. Since she was three hours away from her mom, the ladies in that church were her advisers on how to raise her son. They were like mothers and sisters to her even the men were her fathers that she respected, and the young men were her brothers. When she had questions they always had an answer. From the very beginning she brought her son home all the way up to his toddler years. They came to her house for three or four hours to show her how to change the baby's diaper, how to burp, how to put the baby to sleep, etc. She really depended on them for their experience and support. They even brought them food since they were unable to cook as much. Amy felt very blessed. She knew not many moms had this total support. She loved those ladies so much.

Amy stopped working for at least nine months which drastically lowered their income. Amy and her husband were not willing to acquire a baby sitter or Day Care. She knew this time was precious for her son. Amy had no choice but to sell her investment property in Pennsylvania that she had worked so hard to keep so they could have some money to pay the bills. When Amy was not working due to maternity leave their income was cut by more than a half. The property was one Amy had bought when she was single, and she had kept it for seven years. She had no problem paying for the mortgage until she married her husband. Since they paid for two mortgages, the property in Pennsylvania and the one that they bought as their first home in New York, it caused them to have more bills than savings.

Amy was disappointed so many times that she wondered if she had made the right decision. But since she had already said her wedding vows there was no turning back. Over time, Amy learned to love her husband through thick and thin, but she didn't appreciate the way she felt she was lured into marrying him. Her hope for him to get that good job never came true. It became a huge struggle throughout their marriage and also to Amy's parents. Amy learned from that experience that she couldn't really trust anyone, even her own pastor. In the end, she became the bread winner in her family.

One day the two-faced pastor made a troubling comment to Amy about her husband. He said, "Smart people like him like to argue." This proved to Amy that she was not always in the wrong. But if he had known this why didn't he tell her before? There was no use in thinking about it or bringing it up now.

AMY KEPT HERSELF active in the church, not because it was the only thing she knew to do but because of her strong faith in God. She believed that churches should be known for sharing the gospel and doing good like helping the poor, so she was convinced that's where they should stay.

In those good years they had scheduled their lives around every ministry the church provided; Sunday was church, Wednesday was Prayer Meeting, Friday was Bible Study, and Saturday Choir Practice. During holidays like Christmas and Easter they were at church almost every day helping to decorate, clean up and practice for the concert. Many were in that church so much that one would think that even the pastor lived his sermon every day. He would make others think that he really loved God and was devoted to His Word.

Many missionaries and pastors visited their church, encouraging them in their walk with the Lord, to do their devotions and constantly pray to God for He is their purpose in life. But when her pastor preached, Amy's mind wandered off, thinking, *How can this man live with himself? How could he use God's name and do this kind of action leading to spiritual havoc?*

The whole time they attended that church as a married couple they never went to him for any marriage counseling. Because either he was always away traveling, or, most of all, his walk didn't match up with his talk. Amy often just talked to one of her trusted friends in the church. If she wasn't available, she called up her sister. But even then, a pastor should always avail himself for his flock to protect and care for them and most importantly help them grow spiritually.

WHILE ATTENDING THE church, Amy learned a few things about the pastor's past life; His mom died when he was ten years old and ever since then his family had been a wreck. His father worked for the U.S. Army in the Philippines, so he wasn't home a lot to care for all his children, two boys and two girls. He was the second oldest. This pastor failed a couple of times in school and had to redo some grades again.

Sometimes during his sermons, he told the church that he used to abuse and deal drugs in the Philippines. He was arrested for Drug Trafficking. He loved basketball and Word of Life Bible Institute happened to have a basketball ministry. It was there that he heard about the gospel; Although, he was a Hindu first before attending church.

Later in life he went to Bible Baptist Seminary and Institute to become a pastor. Even while attending Bible Baptist Seminary he and his friends did drugs. His group was a very rowdy bunch playing pranks and jokes on each other. For example, while he was in the bathroom his friends took a picture of his private part. They all laughed at it, finding no fault with this humor. Also, while in the seminary there was a visiting Missionary. One of the staff caught this pastor making out with her. As a result, he and his friends did not graduate. Apostle Paul says this about growing in Christ in I Corinthians 13:11—When I was a child, I talked like a child, I thought like a child, I reasoned like a child. When I became a man, I put the ways of childhood behind me. There has to be a change in the way we talk, walk and think after we accept Christ in our heart. It may not be immediate. Ephesians 4:22-24—That, in reference to your former manner of life, you lay aside the old self, which is being corrupted in accordance with the lusts of deceit, and that you be renewed in the spirit of your mind, and put on the new self, which in the likeness of God has been created in righteousness and holiness of the Truth. Romans 6:6—Knowing this, that our old man is crucified with him, that the body of sin might be destroyed, that henceforth we should not serve sin. Galatians 5:16-18— This I say then, walk in the Spirit, and ye shall not fulfill the lust of the flesh. For the flesh lusteth against the Spirit, and the Spirit against the flesh: and these are contrary the one to the other: so that ye cannot do the things that ye would. But if ye be led of the Spirit, ye are not under the law.

He was suspended from that Bible School and was placed under a pastor who was known to restore and help struggling Christians, students that did not graduate including pastors. He was under his guidance for about two years helping out in the church ministries like Bible Studies. He met his wife there, and this was also where his son and daughter were born. He eventually let Pastor Janus lead that church without him being ordained.

What is Ordination? According to the teaching of the New Testament, ordination is the recognition by the local church of a member's call of God to the gospel ministry. The recognition consists of the candidate's conversion to Christ, his call to the ministry, and his conviction of beliefs. Ordination does not confer any ecclesiastical power, it gives no authority, nor does it confer status to the ordained member of the church.

Since ordination does involve other churches and the candidate's future ministry, the ordaining church has responsibility not to lay hands suddenly or lightly on any man. There should be a very careful and prayerful searching inquiry made into the candidate's experience of grace, the reality of his conversion, his call, his character, the worthiness of his concept of his call and his loyalty to Christ and the church. After all, he will be the representative of the church which ordains him.

Must the Pastor Be Ordained? The simple answer is no. Ordination is not a requirement that must be met in order to preach.

There is a scriptural basis for ordination. The Lord Jesus chose a select group of men whom He "ordained" or "appointed" to be his special representatives (John 15:16; Mark 3:14). There was evidently an ordination service of some sort held at the church at Antioch for Paul and Barnabas (Acts 13:2, 3). Paul and Barnabas also ordained elders in the churches (Acts 14:23). Paul commanded Titus to ordain elders or pastors (Titus 1:5). Thus there is a scriptural basis for ordination. As a rule, ordination should not take place until a man has been called to a definite place of service and has had time to prove himself.

This article is from Dr. Elmer Towns, a college and seminary professor. His education includes a B.S. from Northwestern College in Minneapolis, Minnesota, a M.A. from Southern Methodist University in Dallas,

Texas, a Th.M. from Dallas Theological Seminary also in Dallas, a MRE from Garrett Theological Seminary in Evanston, Illinois and a D.Min. from Fuller Theological Seminary in Pasadena, California.

H IS GUIDANCE PASTOR decided to branch out and open another church while he let him lead that church in Manila, Philippines. It was actually at least 10 years later when Pastor Janus received his diploma from the Victory In Jesus Seminary. Years later, Janus's true identity confirmed he was a master manipulator, deceiver who had false humility and a Jekyll/Hyde persona. The guidance pastor did not judge his motivation then but trusted God that whatever Janus decided to do would be his own responsibility.

Later on, Janus came to America. He went first before his wife and his kids, when he attended a Pastors' Conference. At that time, he wasn't yet a U.S. citizen until the church petitioned him. Their kids eventually grew up in the United States and both went to college after high school graduation; One took English Lit and the other Counselor Education.

So, his family was blessed in a lot of ways when he became a pastor; However, sometimes between sermons he behaved as if the church didn't pay him enough. He didn't directly ask for money, but he told stories to make people pity them. In the beginning the only reason why he didn't get paid much was because the church was still small and not getting enough offering. But by 2010 his income was up to $52,000, not counting private gifts people gave him and all the pastoral benefits such as air travel, educational, housing, phone, electricity, (car and life) insurance, internet, cable, cell, tolls and gas expense. As one of his relatives said, he had a way of asking for money instead of working hard for it and being frugal in his living.

Many of the church members paid horrendous mortgages or rent on their houses, while the pastor lived for free, with outstanding pastoral benefits and free utilities plus Ministry account. Amy just could not understand how they could not save any money. As a married woman now, she struggled to pay their bills and mortgage, but they were never bold enough to ask anyone for money.

AMY AND HER husband loved being at that church because they enjoyed fellowshipping with the people. There was a thrill of excitement about being together because they had genuine love for each other compared to many churches that didn't share that Christ-like love. The bond they had with each other was strong. This was not the type of church that lacked deep connections between families, where hardly anyone hugged, joined to celebrate a special occasion such as a birthday, wedding, bridal shower, birthday party, anniversary, baby dedication etc., or where people just came to church because it was Sunday or Wednesday because it was Prayer Meeting.

Amy treasured every memory she had with the people in that church, in spite of knowing in the back of her mind that she had to watch out for the pastor and keep his secret life quiet. She was certain that her children were going to be raised there all their lives, but apparently God had a different plan.

One day after Amy and her husband returned from visiting Amy's parents in Lancaster, Pennsylvania, they overheard that the pastor's son had gotten a girl pregnant. She was in her early 20s and was so close to finishing up her degree in college. Her dad was a well-known pastor too in Korea. It was a big shock in her church and everyone was caught off guard.

The pastor and his wife asked the church for forgiveness. Praise God the church was more than willing to forgive them and soon the problem quieted down. Eventually, the pastor's son and the young lady did get married when she was approximately seven months pregnant. They got divorced years later.

A YEAR LATER Mark and Amy had a Baby Dedication for their son with loving godfathers and godmothers that prayed faithfully for him. Her husband and she chose the godparents according to their spiritual maturity. Those godparents gave their son presents every year and spoiled him with lots of hugs and kisses whenever they saw him.

Birthday parties were frequently celebrated with other children. All the family had to do was bring a birthday cake. After lunch everyone sang the Happy Birthday song in unity. Then the pastor or a deacon prayed for the child. Some of the ladies helped cut and hand out the cake. Many went so far as to bring prizes, to play games, and even provide a piñata for the children. It was a place where a kid could be a kid. Life in that church was almost too good to be true. It was the kind of church where the people that attended were family, and everyone celebrated special occasions together. They had very fond and happy memories of the people in that church. Many pictures and videos were taken of things that happened. It was unforgettable.

ONE DAY, AMY looked to buy her adopted dad a watch for his birthday. The two-faced pastor encouraged her to go to New York City to buy a Rolex. At first, Amy and her husband were a little hesitant, knowing that everything in NYC is expensive. But then the pastor told them watches were only $10 in Chinatown. They were in disbelief and wondered if this was even legal.

However, they went, and a friend dropped them off in the busy section of Chinatown. Not knowing how to ask or where to go Amy and her husband looked around where they sell the watches. They sheepishly asked the shopkeepers if they sold any Rolex watches. The shopkeeper hushed them and then led them away from the crowd.

Amy and her husband looked through the collection of watches but were undecided if they should go on. Since this was the pastor's idea, though, they bought a watch that looked like a genuine Rolex. And yet why did they feel so guilty? How illegal could this be? Why was the Rolex so cheap? It was the first Rolex watch they ever bought and it was also the last.

Amy's dad did like the watch very much, and when it broke years later he took it to a repair shop to get it fixed. However, the watch repairman was surprised to find out that it only cost $10 when it looked so much like a genuine Rolex. Was it stolen? No, it was a replica or a bootleg that was probably made at a forced labor camp. So, yes, it was still illegal.

Rumor had it that their pastor would buy a lot of these Rolex watches from Chinatown and bring them to the Philippines. Should a pastor be a part of this dealing? Probably not. God watches everything that we do.

B Y NOW THEY were married for a while. And since Mark was Pastor Janus's godson, one of his jobs was to pick him up at the airport. So, Amy went with Mark. As they got there her husband dropped her off at the arrival area to look for him while her husband stayed in the car.

After looking around she went downstairs. As she went around the corner, she happened to catch her pastor staring at a woman dressed very elegant and sexy. His eyes were fixed on her so steadfastly as if mesmerized while standing there motionless.

Amy was tempted to video record or even take a picture because what she saw seemed unbelievable. She knew his wife waited outside while he was inside eyeing another woman. She was aware of the time and she knew that he stared at her long enough. She had to break his concentration. She could tell the woman felt uncomfortable.

So, Amy approached him saying out loud, "Pastor! Pastor!" and gave him a warm happy hug. She greeted him trying not to sound or look shocked. She then looked at the lady and tried to find out if there was any friendship between them, but they acted like two strangers.

She then walked him and his wife to where Mark was parked. She felt the whole situation was very bizarre but again she tried to shrug it off.

AMY AND HER husband were faithful churchgoers by this time but had never seriously considered church membership. Since Amy felt like she had no voice in that church, had never whole-heartedly trusted the pastor and had no peace in her heart with what was happening in that church, she dismissed the idea of becoming a member. Even though many people tried to persuade them to join, they refused. Those people didn't know what Amy and her husband had in mind.

Amy was active in many ministries and had made many close friends among the women. While many ladies had preferred groups of friends or cliques Amy was a friend to all. It didn't matter how they looked, what color or what kind of personality they were, she always greeted them with an open mind and heart. One of the women brought up to Amy the idea of a ladies' gathering once a month, so she approached one of the members in charge of it. She humbly encouraged her that they should have it every month instead of every six months. The leader considered it for a while and decided to pass the leadership to Amy. Although Amy was not expecting her decision to turn out like that, she took her offer seriously.

Amy started Ladies Fellowship which was held one Saturday each month. She picked ladies up from their homes and dropped them off. The most that came were about 20 ladies and the least was one. But rain or shine with God's help Amy kept the ministry going for almost two years, until they scheduled another person to take her place while she was away on vacation. They did not tell Amy their decision nor explain what they thought she did wrong. Even though their decision hurt her, God told her to let it go. So, she moved on.

A MY ALSO BROUGHT up the Door Knocking Track Distribution, which she started with a missionary's help. She saw the need in her community of people looking for help but looking in a different place, and she knew that church was the key to steering families in the right direction. A lot of people from the church came to Door Knocking Track Distribution including children and teenagers, but Amy noticed the most important leader, the pastor, was not there. It was very puzzling to her. Later on, she found out that the reason why he didn't come to any Door Knocking Ministry was because to him this ministry was not an official ministry.

So Amy looked up the meaning of the word "official." Official means having the approval or authorization of an authority or public body. Some synonyms are authorized, approved, validated, etc. She then compared this definition to what the Bible has to say. Jesus had already authorized Christians several times in the New Testament to go into all the world to make disciples. Sadly, the Great Commission has been the "great omission." Churches must have a fire for evangelism and since many Christians are unlikely to share the gospel and faith to their neighbors, Door Knocking Track Distribution had opened that opportunity. It should have been the highest responsibility and ministry of the church. Was the pastor encouraging this ministry? No, he never even tried. As a matter of fact, he had more ministries overseas than ministries in his own backyard. Jehovah's Witnesses are more faithful about this ministry than Born Again Christians. After the ministry Amy and her husband provided food for all the volunteers out of their own pocket.

Then approximately two years later Amy started another ministry for graduating high school students who left for college and were not heard from for several years. Amy thought that was a sad thing, so she had a celebration for them before they left. They gave each graduate a small Gideon Bible to take with them to college and, before the party ended, Amy assigned them with a prayer partner from the church. This was the most important event of all. This way, these young adults would not be forgotten while they were away from home and would be remembered in prayers and thoughts. Later, this ministry was turned to another person in the church who changed the name to Baccalaureate.

M EANWHILE, ANOTHER FAMILY of five started coming to the church. Their children were all very talented and obedient. One day the parent got offended over minor things, so they wanted to have a meeting with Amy. But the real problem was that the pastor chose not to be the mediator. So, to them, there was no solution or even reconciliation in their dilemma, even though Amy did apologize to them in order to appease the situation.

In the end, they left the church because of the pastor who did not want to get involved. They felt that Pastor Janus sided with her since they knew each other. The pastor should have been the mediator rather than breaking the Christian relationship. Isn't that one of the pastor's jobs?

The latest family Amy learned that left was a family of five. The father was a deacon for several years and faithfully maintained the church property. They had three young children although the couple had been there even before they dated. They too did not agree with the leadership or the vision of the church.

Not once did the pastor try to reach out to any of these faithful members. Many of them disappeared with wounds still open, wounds that took years to heal. Many others left the church; These were just a few.

While many attended, and many left the church, it was hard for the church to double or triple in size because of the leadership structure. So, for the most part, the reasons why people left the church were because they didn't like how the leadership was handled, they were not growing spiritually anymore, and, most importantly, because of the pastor.

First Meeting

O FF AND ON Amy Stiles overheard people say in the church that Pastor Janus gave massages to ladies but never heard the details until years later; Details that confirmed he did it alone in their rooms, touching them on their legs, backs and shoulders. It became very troubling, but she never heard the pastor apologize to the church. Some may have been afraid to approach the pastor and the deacons since they seemed like a very close-knit group. But once Amy was married she hoped to have more backup or support.

In her mind, all these factors were adding up as inappropriate behavior, a bad example and a definite wrong in a Christian and non-Christian perspective.

So, she decided to have a meeting with the pastor and with that she made a list of things that bothered her about him, knowing that if she didn't make a list she might easily forget due to fears. So, Amy had about 13 things she wanted to ask the pastor.

B EFORE APPROACHING THE pastor, Amy decided to seek assurance with one of the faithful ladies in the church to see if these were important things to bring up to him. She decided if this woman felt it was petty then she would probably just drop the whole subject and move on with life. Amy chose the choir director, who had been a Christian for a very long time, had attended Word of Life Bible Institute and had a history of being sexually abused as a child. If anyone would understand it would be her.

She said, "These are hurts. You should bring it up to him." These were her verbatim words. Amy was encouraged more to confront the pastor despite her nervousness towards him. So, Amy decided that this meeting was a necessity. It took a while to finally speak to the pastor privately. She had knocked on his door a couple of times and called him on the phone but there was no response. When she finally did meet (several weeks later) the choir director volunteered to accompany her to meet with him in the fellowship hall.

During the meeting, the three of them were alone and Amy nervously opened her paper and made sure her tone of voice was not showing any anger or disrespect.

She timidly told the pastor, "I don't think it's a good idea to be taking single ladies out to lunch or places alone."

His reply was, "That's how I counsel them."

(Looking back at the situation, Amy couldn't recall him counseling her when he took her out alone to many places.) She cautioned him, "What if someone sees you? The Bible says, 'Stay away from appearance of evil.'"

"That verse doesn't go with this situation." He acted very bossy.

Feeling intimidated, Amy quieted down. She thought if that was true then there are many other verses that tell us to stay away from the appearance of evil, such as 2 Timothy 2:22, 1 Timothy 6:11 living as blamelessly as possible, 1 Timothy 3:2 and walking carefully and wisely, and Ephesians 5:15-17, but since she didn't want to argue she let it go.

Next question: "Is it true that you massage young ladies alone in a room, like Trisha? The Bible says, 'It's better for a man not to touch a woman.'"

"That Bible verse applies to marriage, not this situation," he sternly said. "Besides, I needed money."

Shocked by his answer Amy replied, "But how can you need money when the church is paying you faithfully, you're living for free in the parsonage including free utilities, and your wife is a nurse?"

Amy had only gotten to about three questions when the pastor started getting upset. She wondered what she had done wrong. The pastor accused her of being bitter and so she checked her reputation. People knew Amy as a meek and friendly person. But now the pastor falsely accused her of being bitter, and she was troubled. The pastor made Amy feel so badly about making him upset that she apologized to him and even gave him a hug.

This was a man of God that got upset because she brought up things that had affected the church for many, many years. Numerous people knew about these things but were just too afraid to ask.

AMY LEFT THE meeting feeling intimidated. She felt she should have just listened to all that he said and should have never asked questions regarding his behavior. Yet at the same time Amy had this inner feeling of boldness to stand up against the wrong. She was more than willing to try to understand his view, but his view just did not make sense. From a Christian perspective it was definitely confusing not biblical.

The meetings made her lose a lot of sleep, and she couldn't stop wondering what she had done wrong. When a person was left troubled like that she knew it sometimes was not right.

The choir director concluded the meeting by saying, "We cannot change a person, only God can do that." But her statement troubled Amy. Doesn't God also use people to change others? In the Bible, God used people like Noah, Paul, Samson and many others to fulfill his plan. God doesn't want anyone to ignore sin or turn a blind eye; The Bible says in James 4:17, "Therefore to him that knoweth to do good and doeth it not, to him it is sin." Amy knew this kind of sin should not happen in church. It had to be stopped or else it would affect the spiritual growth of every believer there.

Years later, Amy learned that one of the young ladies whom the pastor frequently massaged was still a baby Christian at the time, so she may not have known that what the pastor did to her was inappropriate or a bad example for a pastor to set. She was, after all, very young (in her 20s), single, and away from home, and she looked up to the pastor as a father figure.

Yet even then in Amy's own life she would never have let her own father touch her in such an intimate area, which showed Amy just how manipulative, cunning, and persuasive the pastor was. He had a way of making people go against their natural instinct.

On Sundays following that unbelievable and troublesome meeting, the two-faced pastor started to snub Amy. She tried to make conversation with him but all he would say was "Hi". She took it in stride, thinking she had been treated much worse in her past and could live with this.

Then the pastor started to snub Amy's husband, who came home and said, "They don't talk to me anymore." This caused many troubled days and sleepless nights when Amy knew a pastor should be setting an example rather than making the situation worse.

And he did make it worse by mistreating Amy's son, which was the worst thing you could do to a mother. Amy and her husband put up with the pastor's snobbery and bad attitude for three years while he tried to find more ways to crumble them.

AROUND 2012, THE pastor and his wife traveled to the Philippines because she decided to get surgery done there since it was cheaper. The hospital that performed her operation was not renowned, and unfortunately, they had to do the surgery twice due to complications. But then, unexpectedly, the pastor too had to have major surgery due to an acquired, internal injury to his one kidney. A life and death situation, the doctor had to remove it. The family by this time had spent a lot of money and was now asking relatives and church members for financial help.

Mark and Amy, despite the pastor's treatment towards them, volunteered to bring the money from his aunts here in America to the Philippines. When they got there, they were shocked to see that the pastor stayed in the very prestigious hospital, much like one in the United States but far better in terms of service, care, etc., earning the title one of the "Best Hospitals Worldwide."

Traveling for Amy and her husband was free since they worked for the airline, so they endured the 18-hour flight in order to help. When they saw the pastor, he was still very weak and confined to bed. After a while, he talked to them about how great the hospital was. He said things like, "This is the only hospital in the Philippines that Cobra insurance will take, and they only hire the best doctors and the best nurses here…" etc. So, Amy added up all his comments and asked him blatantly, "So you came here but your wife went somewhere else?" It didn't seem to make sense to her. If it was as good as he said, why did he not bring his wife there too?!

He also talked to them about their home church back in the States. He said the lead singer constantly sang modern worship songs instead of hymnal songs which from his voice he didn't really approve of. Amy considered this gossiping. If he had a problem with his church leader he should have discussed it with him not with them. They had no control over what was happening in church; Only him. Amy knew the family really well and they were great friends, but for him to talk about the singer like that disgusted her.

Despite Amy and Mark's big favor for the pastor and his family, they were still very indifferent towards them in the church.

A MY'S HUSBAND TALKED about switching churches long before this for many reasons: One, because he didn't like the way this pastor was treating them. They were more like strangers to them than a family. Two, most of the time he didn't agree with the pastor's preaching; Therefore, he wasn't growing spiritually anymore. All he wanted to do was leave. But then something in Amy decided to seek counsel from other pastors close by regarding the pastor's behavior towards women (without mentioning his name).

The two local pastors were both appalled that a pastor of the area massaged and took out ladies alone. These pastors encouraged Amy to have a meeting with the deacons to see what the leadership had to say regarding their pastor. As far as they were concerned those things should not have been happening at all. When Amy told them who it was they could not accept that it was one of their dearest and closest friends.

Even before the meeting date was planned some of the deacons in Amy's church already belittled her and arrogantly predicted that her marriage would crumble because of the situation. Another said that she made serious accusations. Another texted her stating, "If you don't agree with our pastor then you are just hindering the church from growing" and suggested she was being a discouragement to them. But one deacon boldly said, "We must hear Amy out. If she has a concern, we should be able to listen." Even though he was the youngest one in the bunch he seemed more knowledgeable of what the Bible had to say about handling problems.

Second Meeting

S O, IN FEBRUARY of 2015, on a Saturday morning at 8 a.m., the meeting was scheduled. Amy Stiles planned to bring several pastors and many witnesses with her, because she knew she had the upper hand. There was no way she could lose. But when she asked the two pastors that she sought for counsel, they said they were busy, stating, "Since this is an internal matter it should be handled within the church." Consequently, the pastors' absence naturally frightened the witnesses and they also didn't come. Amy went alone because she couldn't persuade them.

A family man who used to attend the church said to her, "You're going to lose if you don't bring someone with you." Even though he believed in Amy and knew she was doing the right thing he could already predict from experience what was going to happen. But what could Amy do? She could only trust in her God who makes no mistakes.

With her husband home babysitting their two young children, she bravely went to the meeting. She never forced her husband to come; She figured if he really wanted to come to support her, he would do everything and anything to find a way to accompany her. She knew she had Christ on her side and that was enough.

The deacons let Amy talk first at the meeting. Six deacons were at the front and the pastor and his wife were on the other side. She was not afraid. These were the exact words she said to the deacons:

Amy: (reading from the paper she had typed the night before) *I came to this church in my early 20s because of my job. Church was like second nature to me. My parents took me to a conservative church every Sunday morning and evening. So when I moved here I knew finding a church was essential. I found this church in a Yellow Book and called them up hoping there would be a van ministry—someone to pick me up. I was a country girl and was ignorant of city transportation.*

There were many people who picked me up but one of them was Pastor Janus. I figured since he is the pastor he would know a lot of people to accompany us— his wife, children or friends. Many times, he was alone. Of course, I'd feel uneasy and uncomfortable— something my heart wasn't agreeing to. He took me to the mall. He took me to a fine restaurant and even to NYC but none of that was for counseling. There was one time I needed advice, but I met him in the parsonage.

Then he offered me a massage one day. I hesitated, and I stopped going to church for a while. When my unsaved friends would ask me if I knew anyone who can give massages, I told them that my pastor can. They laughed and thought it was funny. I then realized if the unsaved know it's not right how much more for us Christians? This should not be happening in a church, but I was afraid to confront him.

Years went by; I got married and had children. Then I heard from someone else that he took many other single ladies out to lunch/dinner and places alone too— like Janice, another flight attendant, Elsa, Emily, Marlene and Mae. Also, I overheard that he gave massages to many young ladies in the church, like Emily and Trisha, sometimes alone in a room. So, I knew it was time to confront him. I was hearing too much and me coming from a conservative church—I knew this should not be happening.

This happened about three years ago. I confronted him along with the choir director.

I said to him, "Is it true that you give massages to young, single ladies like Trisha alone in a room?" I gave verses to back up my point which is, "It's better for a man not to touch a woman."

His reply was, "I needed money."

I also told him that it's not a good idea to be taking young ladies out to lunch/dinner alone because what if someone sees you? Bible verse: Abstain from appearance of evil.

His answer: I was counseling them. I never got to ask him all the things I had written down because he accused me of being bitter. He also said that the verses I mentioned did not apply to him.

Moreover, he got mad at the choir director because this should have been a one-on-one discussion, but I was glad the choir director was there to accompany me. It was more appropriate. Why would I want to be alone with him anyway especially with his background? There was no solution to the meeting since he got upset.

Feeling fearful, I apologized to him after the confrontation and gave him a hug thinking that it was all over but Sundays after that he became snobbish towards my husband and me. We would greet him, but he would only say Hi. Even my husband would say that he doesn't talk to him anymore. I know what I did was right and biblical but now his attitude was wrong. I knew this was not a trait of a true pastor.

I tried to go on with life, although the answers he gave me left me bewildered. The more I tried to forget it the more it haunted me, as if God didn't want me to forget it. I started to ask questions of my Christian friends, such as, was this appropriate behavior for a pastor to massage and take ladies out? I went up higher and asked lots of pastors. Most of them would tell me it's not right. A pastor should not do these kinds of things. It's a bad testimony. It makes the church look bad. In I Peter 5:1-4 The elders which are among you I exhort, who am also an elder, and a witness of the suffering of Christ and also a partaker of the glory that shall be revealed. Feed the flock of God which is among you, taking the oversight thereof not by constraint but willingly not FILTHY LUCRE but of a ready mind. Neither as being lords over God's heritage but being examples to the flock. And when the chief Shepherd shall appear, ye shall receive a crown of glory that fadeth not away.

I explained to them that filthy lucre is dishonest gain. These terms are used five times in the New Testament and in each case refer to ministers. "Gain," "Lucre," that is money is not bad but if it is "filthy or dishonest," that is obtained in a dishonest or dishonorable manner it is, according to Bible Gateway website. This pastor gained money through massaging. He lured ladies into saying, "It's okay. I can be your father figure—there's nothing wrong with this idea." So, these ladies came to him when deep down they knew it was wrong. This manner is definitely dishonorable to God.

In verse 3 the sentence, "but being ensamples to the flock" means instead of ruling imperiously, rather set an example that others may follow. Is Pastor Janus's action something we should follow? After I apologized to him he still held grudges for years and ignored us, when he should be approachable, merciful and forgiving about any issues and have a Christ-like attitude.

Lastly, what really ticked me off was what happened recently during a family reunion. All the relatives were in the church. All the cousins were running around playing. Out of the blue, my son was pulling me towards the kitchen. At first, I was annoyed because I was talking to someone but then I gave in to my son.

Pastor Janus saw me and said, "Amy, he was playing with the matches."

I humbly told him that we don't have matches at home. He doesn't know what matches look like.

His shocking reply was, "Well, he could have burned the whole church down." Appalled by his comment, I still bit my tongue because this time he had crossed the line. But he kept going, "See all he had to do was open this box, take a match out and slide it." He did the whole demonstration right in front of me and my son. But being a good Christian, I didn't argue back. I just listened.

I also noticed a red mark on my son's neck. So, I asked my son, "Who did this to you?" He pointed his finger at Pastor Janus and said, "That old man."

That same day, the relatives hung out in the parsonage. My son was playing with his cousins. Kids were going to be kids. They fought and became friends again. So, I heard door slamming and someone crying. I went over towards the crying area. I was about eight months pregnant then with swollen legs, arms and face. I had difficulty walking much less chasing my son around.

Pastor Janus's wife said, "Your son did this and that!"

So, I gently said to my son, "You have to say sorry and give her a hug." So, he did it without hesitation.

But then the aunt was being belligerent and said, "You need to put him on time-out or palo him!!!" meaning spank him.

I told her accidents do happen, but she continued to be mad. What's worse was that Pastor Janus stood right beside her yet didn't say a thing. Isn't a pastor supposed to be a peacemaker?

I decided to leave that place at that hour bringing my son with me. I was exhausted from being around people that call themselves Christian, but this is how they act. "Such hypocrites," I said to myself.

That evening I was really troubled and frustrated, so I called my mom for support. She said Pastor Janus should have never made a big deal out of it. He should have just put the matches away. Besides, whoever put the matches there was the one at fault. They should have never been where the kids could have reached them.

Pastor Janus never came up to me to apologize for the hurt he caused. Now we no longer have enthusiasm going to church. It has become a drag, almost a chore. When we deeply love the people in this church, but the pastor is being... So now I would like to know where you guys stand in this matter. Should a pastor massage and take ladies out?

A MY STOPPED READING the paper that she wrote and listened to what the deacons had to say. The deacons from Victory United didn't allow her to get a copy of the recording even though she was part of the meeting. They said it was church property. So, these conversations were her recollection of the events that happened during the three to four-hour meeting. They did not tell Amy that the pastor was going to be there.

All the deacons said was that there would be a meeting with the board.

List of Deacons:

#1 Mark—hot tempered, Pro-Pastor
#2 James—made no comments throughout the whole entire meeting. He just sat there quietly. Pro-Pastor
#3 Larry—Youth Leader
#4 Kevin—the Mediator during the meeting, Pro-Pastor
#5 Vince—Choir Director's husband, Pro-Pastor
#6 Daniel—baby Christian, Pro-Pastor

#6 Deacon: *I don't mind Pastor massaging.*
(Then Pastor brought in a recording and it was of the young lady that he used to massage alone in a room several years ago. She said, he did massage her, but no sexual thing happened between them.)
Pastor: *I stopped massaging four years ago.*
Amy: *He never told me that, otherwise this would have been a totally different story.*
Pastor: *She only knows two people that I massaged. I massaged both genders, not just women. Remember Mr. H, he used to have health problems and he'd ask me to massage him. There was no evil intention.*
[Amy's thoughts: He's trying to make himself look good. Just because I only know two young ladies that he massaged, as if two isn't enough.]
#4 Deacon: *Did you get a massage from him?*
Amy: *No, I would never let him touch me!*

Pastor: *I do take ladies out socially. There are times when they ask me to take them to places, like Julie (non-churchgoer and non-believer), another flight attendant who wanted me to take her some place which was an hour drive. Another lady in the church asked me if I could see her. She needed to talk to me. So, I called her husband first to see if it was okay.*

Amy: *He never asked me if it was okay to see me alone.*

Pastor: *Well, you didn't have a husband.*

[Amy's thoughts: Is this a good character trait of a pastor? I don't think so. Just because I don't have a husband doesn't give him the right to take me or anyone out alone.]

Pastor's wife: *She has called my husband like 100 times.*

[Amy's thoughts: If that was true why didn't she do anything to stop me? This was a total over exaggeration and false statement.]

Pastor: *As a matter of fact, there was a choir group picture we took one time and her head was leaning on my shoulder.*

[He was giving an inkling that I misbehaved. But I'd rather lean my head on him as if he was my father than touch him on legs, back and shoulders like he does with some of these ladies.]

#4 Deacon: *So, is it true that the aunties yelled at her during the family reunion?*

Pastor: *Yeah, because they were telling her how to raise her kids, but she was walking away.*

#4 Deacon: *So, Amy has a relational problem?*

Pastor: *Yeah.*

[Amy's thoughts: What kind of conclusion is that when that deacon doesn't even know me?]

Pastor: *The P. family left the church because of Amy.*

[Amy's thoughts: He's trying hard to make me look bad again, accusing me of things that are irrelevant. Plus, he's lying. The family he mentioned left because of him. He refused to be the mediator for a meeting.]

#4 Deacon: *Is it true about her son and the matches?*

Pastor: *Yes. He was playing with the matches. The reason why I feel strongly about children and matches is because it happened before with another kid that I babysat who almost burned down the parsonage. He liked playing with matches too.*

[Amy's thoughts: I was there when that happened. The boy played with the matches because he was left in the kitchen unsupervised when the pastor should have been babysitting him. But the pastor was in the computer room going online. When I came back the little boy was furiously crying. Apparently, Pastor Janus did something to him to make him cry. The family said their son does not play with fire but Pastor Janus accused the child of enjoying it. He spread that rumor to other people in the church. So much that anyone who greeted the family brought up the subject labeling him 'the boy who almost burnt down the parsonage'. The little boy was only six years old and I was sure if Pastor Janus's grandson were responsible, he wouldn't spread false rumors, lie, or mistreat him like he did that little boy. He created an atmosphere of prejudice against the family instead of an atmosphere of love and forgiveness. The parents felt bad about what had happened but the

church didn't make it easier. The mother was brought to tears and the father carried a burden of shame. When I came back from my errands Pastor Janus tried to shift the blame on me asking me where I was. I looked at him dumbfounded. I was at the airport. It was not my business to stay. This pastor seems to think that instead of taking responsibility, blaming someone else is optimal. Instead of apologizing, he would rather someone else look bad. As a result, the heartbroken family withdrew from the church eventually leaving it altogether.]

#5 Deacon: *Maybe the reason why your son had a mark on his neck was because he accidently got some of the red matches on himself.*

[Amy's thoughts: Why is it that they constantly cover up for him? The deacon's job is to find out the Truth not to make up or assume the Truth.]

Pastor: *She has this young man come to her house to babysit her kids.*

#3 Deacon: *What's that have to do with this situation?*

Pastor: *It's called a double-standard.*

[Amy's thoughts: My kids are always with me wherever I go, unlike him. Only one time an illustrator went to Dunkin Donuts with me. We discussed my future children's book. In my home it would have been too chaotic with my two kids, children playing, but in a quiet setting it was more professional. There was no touching involved, no massaging. Besides, I'm not a pastor. A pastor must set an example at all times.]

#3 Deacon: *How many questions did Amy ask you during the first meeting?*

Pastor: *She had like 26 questions on her paper.*

[Amy's thoughts: Over-exaggeration! I had approximately 13, but I only got to ask him three questions. This man has no problem lying and twisting stories.]

Pastor: *Amy asked me to meet her in the parsonage alone for advice about her father in the Philippines. Her father did a terrible crime.*

[Amy's thoughts: My father should have never been mentioned in this meeting. This is totally irrelevant. For the Bible says, II Chronicles 25:3-4 Now it came to pass when the kingdom was established to him (King Amaziah) that he slew his servants that had killed the king his father. But he slew not their children but did as it is written in the law in the book of Moses, where the Lord commanded, saying, The fathers shall not die for the children, neither shall the children die for the fathers, but every man shall die for his own sin. *This pastor has no knowledge about the Bible. To this day I believe that my father is innocent. This pastor doesn't even know my father but talks like a crooked lawyer and spreads rumors. Instead of just apologizing and admitting he is wrong he makes the situation worse.]*

Amy: *I chose the parsonage because there's bound to always be people either upstairs or downstairs.*

[Amy's thoughts: If you ask the many church members there, they'll confirm the parsonage was a hangout place for most of them. The children played games there, karaoke was allowed there, church ministries were held there, it was a meeting place for special

occasions including parties and annual sports games. Privacy was rarely found. And he knows that.]

#4 Deacon: *So, you wanted to meet with pastor alone?*

Amy: *No, I would not have minded if his wife was there. To me the more people, the more advice I could get.*

Pastor: *No, that wasn't what she wanted. She wanted me to meet her alone.*

#4 Deacon: *So, Amy would you consider counseling alone as a "preference" because there are people who prefer doing it alone?*

Amy: (Hesitation) *I guess...*

[Amy's thoughts: I am being harassed and pressured at this time.]

Another Deacon: *Will you return to church now that everything is settled?*

Amy: *I guess so...* (Hesitation)

Pastor: *Well, since she can't listen to my sermons anymore, there's no reason for them to come back. She just said that it's a drag going to church. Besides, the way she talks about me to other pastors, she's slandering me.*

[Amy's thoughts: False accusation. I'm not slandering him. Who says that asking advice from other pastors is slander? When the pastor is not approachable, naturally this will happen. Plus, the Bible speaks about seeking wise counsel.]

Amy: *Isn't it better that I asked people outside the church rather than the people here? Everyone could have known about it.*

#5 Deacon: *Who else have you told this to?*

Another Deacon: *You need to tell us who they are!*

[Amy's thoughts: They are forcing me to tell them who I mentioned this situation to. I wonder what I did wrong. In my mind I only asked advice, but they make me feel like I committed a sin.]

#5 Deacon: *You should apologize to pastor!*

Amy: (Hesitation. *But she decided to do it anyway so that the deacons could see what kind of a person he really was. She knew this man had a dark side to him.*) *Sorry. I didn't confront you before. Next time I will tell you before I go to other pastors.*

Pastor: *You know, Amy, I could have taken you to court.*

Pastor's wife: *You could have lost your job.*

[Amy's thoughts: Shocking, but these are their verbatim words.]

Pastor: *I want her to sign a contract, so she won't talk to anyone about this.*

#3 Deacon: *No. She doesn't have to. Amy is a Word of Life Bible Institute student. We don't allow these things.*

They ended the meeting with a closing prayer. The choir director's husband came up to her immediately and started lecturing her. He said, "You shouldn't let your son call pastor an old man. You shouldn't do this, you shouldn't do that..." Amy walked out of that church trying not to cry.

Another deacon noticed that she was on the verge of tears. He politely asked, "Amy, are you ok?"

"She'll never be happy." Pastor Janus said heartlessly.

HE DENIED A lot of things in the meeting; He refuted accusing Amy of being bitter, her apology to him, and her hug at the first meeting when the choir director was present. He also denied snubbing Amy's husband when his godson was the one that said it. He lied about receiving money for massages. As you can see, this man had no problem lying. But then he didn't deny taking ladies out in a social setting and massaging young ladies. To him there was nothing wrong with what he had done since it wasn't malicious.

Amy really hoped that the meeting would end in a Christ-like way, that her whirling, troubling thoughts of this pastor would soon end and that everyone would soon get along. But after the meeting it got worse. Even with the intervention, the deacons exacerbated things. Amy did not know what she had done wrong, but she felt like she was the one punished and humiliated. She was left rejected, confused, without confidence and hurt.

The same day after the upsetting meeting #4 Deacon texted her husband privately, saying, "I think the pastor was just giving a shoulder massage. If it was a full body massage it would have been a different story." Then the same deacon continued, "If anyone should be upset, it should be his wife."

Amy was outraged that this deacon said all this. He never even verified from other ladies or witnesses if all the things they said were true, yet he was supposed to be the Mediator. There seemed to be no morals in his perspective. He had no fear in God. The people that Amy thought were mature Christians were not mature at all. They all disappointed her, except one young deacon.

AMY LOOKED UP to a lot of women in that church for their love for God, hard work and selfless acts. But she could not understand the pastor's wife, who didn't reflect the same qualities. She knew the events that happened all throughout their married life, yet she didn't do anything about it. Perhaps she was manipulated, but even then, how could one ignore it?

Throughout the whole meeting, the pastor's wife was out of control. She was very angry with Amy and made sure everyone knew about it. She was unruly, constantly talking out of order, staring at her with great hatred, causing many distractions. If looks could kill Amy thought she would have done it. Should this be an attitude of a Christian woman especially a pastor's wife?

At times, we forget that leaders in the church are flesh and blood too who are capable of doing wicked things behind people's backs. They are sometimes the worst culprits because no one suspects them while they are hiding behind the curtain of holiness and religion. People neglect to see that they too can commit hideous crimes, such as child molestation and rape, and that they equally deserve to be locked-up in jail with all the other perverts. We put so much trust in them that we foolishly ignore the cry of our innocent children and other victims who are abused, mind, body and soul.

At the meeting, no one defined the problem or evaluated the results. The deacons based everything on the pastor's wife. If the wife was okay with it, then it should be fine. But what does the Bible instruct believers to do?

A S AMY MADE the list of all the ladies that the pastor took out, she couldn't help but notice that many of them had something in common. The pastor knew exactly which ladies to pick. These ladies were mostly single, away from home, vulnerable and gullible. He knew they couldn't go home and say, "Hey mom and dad, the pastor just gave me a massage today." He knew that their fathers would not permit it. He manipulated the minds of these young ladies when they knew that it was wrong by making them think it was alright.

Not many people knew that Pastor Janus used to go to these single ladies' apartments. Then at 10 pm alone into their rooms; He massaged them in dim lighting while they wore skimpy clothes like sports bras and short shorts putting his hands on their backs, legs and shoulders. Then he left at 1 am. If he didn't find anything wrong with this, then there was something definitely wrong with his head and heart.

One of the missionaries who worked with Pastor Janus in Asia caring for sexually abused girls described him this way: "The boundaries he built to himself as a pastor, a father and a husband are not that high." Amy agreed. He acted as if he was still single, unmarried and had no knowledge of what the Bible says about his behavior. This missionary continued, "I could tell that in his ways in caring these young ladies could lead others to misinterpretation in many ways. Even the recipient of his care could also interpret his ways in a wrong emotional way." She continued, "If I am his child, I would feel not happy with what he is doing because that is not the interpretation of what the Bible said, 'Love your wife,' the pastor knows it, but we can't do anything that's what he chose."

A Stumbling Block

I Corinthians 8: 1-13 KJV—Now as touching things offered unto idols, we know that we all have knowledge. Knowledge puffeth up, but charity edifieth. ²And if any man think that he knoweth any thing, he knoweth nothing yet as he ought to know. ³But if any man love God, the same is known of him. ⁴As concerning therefore the eating of those things that are offered in sacrifice unto idols, we know that an idol is nothing in the world, and that there is none other God but one. ⁵For though there be that are called gods, whether in heaven or in earth, (as there be gods many, and lords many,) ⁶But to us there is but one God, the Father, of whom are all things, and we in him; and one Lord Jesus Christ, by whom are all things, and we by him. ⁷Howbeit there is not in every man that knowledge: for some with conscience of the idol unto this hour eat it as a thing offered unto an idol; and their conscience being weak is defiled. [8] But meat commendeth us not to God: for neither, if we eat, are we the better; neither, if we eat not, are we the worse. [9] But take heed lest by any means this liberty of yours become a stumbling block to them that are weak. [10] For if any man see thee which hast knowledge sit at meat in the idol's temple, shall not the conscience of him which is weak be emboldened to eat those things which are offered to idols; [11] And through thy knowledge shall the weak brother perish, for whom Christ died? [12] But when ye sin so against the brethren, and wound their weak conscience, ye sin against Christ. [13] Wherefore, if meat makes my brother to offend, I will eat no flesh while the world standeth, lest I make my brother to offend.

To summarize all these verses: Paul called the mature Christians to consider the vulnerability of the baby Christians by submitting to their moral sense. The principle of love for the other person surpasses the principle of the personal freedom that comes with faith in Christ.

Amy Stiles had been a Christian for over 20 years and had never imagined in her entire life that a pastor could end up being a stumbling block to her or to anyone when the church spoke about love, unity and grace. Church leaders were there to steer the church in the direction that God was leading, not as dictators. Members and non-members should never fear asking questions of leadership in the church.

AFTER AMY TOLD her husband the result of the meeting, he and Amy had no desire to go back to Victory United. They lost interest in going there because of the way Amy was treated. This time it was definitely official. Who really wants to have a pastor like that? After staying there for so many years Amy realized how much of her spiritual life had been wasted when she should have been growing spiritually for the Lord. She finally realized, too, that the pastor was a wolf in sheep's clothing, a manipulator and not a spiritual leader.

Days after the meeting, Amy called back the two sister church pastors from whom she previously asked for advice. One of them said that the deacons should have established a boundary defining what that pastor could and couldn't do. When Amy told them that the pastor threatened to take her to court for slander, both of them agreed that she was NOT slandering. When she told them the whole story, they were shocked and fully regretted that they did not accompany Amy to the meeting. It was all too late to turn back time.

AS A FLIGHT attendant for over 15 years, passengers always looked at Amy either for assurance and/or out of curiosity. It never once bothered her. But when she went back to work after the meeting she had a totally different perspective of the way men looked at her. So, she wrote this poem:

INTIMIDATED

At times I feel intimidated; the world is watching me.
So many eyes are staring. I'll hide behind a tree.
Is there something on my face—a booger or a snot?
Maybe my hair is a mess; I'll believe you without a
doubt.
I'm very gullible. I'll listen to every word.
Even though what you say is not true at all.
Is my voice funny? I know I've heard much worse.
Can you hear me clearly? I'll slow down my voice.
Some of these guys are scary. What could they be
thinking?
They could be sex offenders: sitting, watching, and
dreaming.
Intimidators can make you feel like you are nothing.
Like wearing no clothes at all in places where people
are walking.
When intimidated you'll feel very ashamed.
Dignity and pride have all been taken away.
Whoever intimidated you knows what he is doing.
He's done this for many years and he will keep on
going.
He is very proud and lacks gentleness.
Because if he had a heart he wouldn't make you
undress.
Usually if they are IN-TI-MI-DA-TORS.
They are also definitely MA-NI-PU-LA-TORS.
So be very aware when you meet someone like that.
Soon they will control the people you love and care
about.

MKG

Amy realized the pastor had affected her mentally in the way she looked at men and life. Before, the way she looked at people was the way Christ looked at us, with love and an open mind. Her motto was: Don't judge a book by its cover. Never judge a person by how they look, talk or walk. Now it seemed that she did not trust anyone after the incident. She hated men especially the controlling type. It effected the way she served at work. She knew she was no longer herself.

Moreover, when she saw her own nationality it brought back bad memories that were too heartbreaking, memories of rejection, betrayal and unfaithful friendship. She realized she had no more desire to be with her own people. Also, she had no more trust for other Christians. Her unconditional love for people had been tarnished. He took away the love she had for people and the pureness of mind. But this song came automatically in her mind.

<u>HIS STRENGTH IS PERFECT</u>
<u>by Steven Chapman</u>

Chorus
His strength is perfect when our strength is gone.
He'll carry us when we can't carry on.
Raised in His power, the weak become strong.
His strength is perfect, His strength is perfect.

Verse I
I can do all things through Christ, who gives me strength.
But sometimes I wonder what He can do through me?

No great success to show, no glory on my own.
Yet in my weakness He is there to let me know.

Verse II
We can only know the power that He holds,
When we truly see how deep our weakness goes.
His strength in us begins, where ours comes to an end,
He hears our humble cry and proves again.

Amy was worn-out physically and spiritually wounded. She thought she was never going to be her old self again. But this song gave her some comfort during those dark, trying times.

S HE ALSO WENT through a stage of fear, not discussing the meeting with anyone. She figured if the pastor did take her to court she would just endanger the financial life of her family by talking. She was quiet for a long time and it became a great burden on her. But then other people began pulling the story out of her mouth little by little, and the more she told people about it the more she realized she had the upper hand. People frequently asked, "How can he sue you?" No one knew the answer. It was then that Amy realized it was the pastor's scare tactic on her. It did work...for a little while.

After Amy left that church it took her four months to finally read her Bible again, because every time she would read or look at her Bible it reminded her of him. The very person that should have set an example and should have had her full trust instead shattered and wounded her spiritually, emotionally, and mentally. He stole the eagerness and enthusiasm she had in her heart for serving Jesus. She didn't know when she was ever going to be active in church ministries again. Anything having to do with church seemed to leave Amy with deep hurt and sadness. Amy did not imagine that a church could leave her feeling so broken. She experienced a roller coaster of emotions that did not come from the Lord. As the saying went, scars did run deep. So, she wrote this poem:

SCARS RUN DEEP

I look at people that I used to know
They were my friends' long time ago.
But when I remembered what they did to me
Scars run deep I still hurt deeply.

I used to hear those lovely songs
Fresh in my mind and encourage me so.
But when I remembered those memories
Scars run deep I still hurt deeply.

When I would pass that certain street
We used to turn there for many years.
But when I remembered the woes and grief
Scars run deep I still hurt deeply.

I used to go to that church long ago
They were a family I treasured so.
But when I remembered how they treated me
Scars run deep I still hurt deeply.

MKG

EVERY SONG AMY sang with the choir on her CD brought a bad taste, resulting in bad memories. How could people sing, "Jesus, I love you," when they just sat back and let their pastor infest the church. Or how could they sing, "You Are My All," when they feared the pastor more than they did God?

The songs that Amy sang in the choir used to fulfill and encourage her, but now they just opened wounds every time she played them in the car or in the house. It was painful remembering the leaders that should have been protecting the flock.

Amy wrote the following poem because she went through a time of isolation where she did not want to meet people or make friends anymore. She lost hope of making friends because of what she had experienced.

ISOLATED

You may see me alone
In the park, coffee restaurant.
In the street, market place,
It's safer to be isolated.
But in a way I like it like that;
At least I know I won't get hurt.
I was a people person before,
Giving my time at all cost.
But the very person that I trusted
The most had me shattered.
Now I don't trust anyone.
Being alone is just grand.
"Leave me alone, please!"
I'll just stay in my comfort place.
The world keeps on going

But I'll stay in my zoning.

MKG

A MY FELT CRIPPLED knowing that everything she had done, both past and present, might be used by the pastor in his sermons to make her look bad. He was known for doing that but since he was the pastor people rarely questioned him or made him stop.

Sure enough, the friends she had at church stopped hanging out with her. She lost most of her friends in the church, since she and her husband were not going back. People that she thought were her friends were not any longer. She felt like an outcast, outsider, rejected and a black sheep. Talk about bring shunned. When she saw them on pictures on Facebook having parties, celebration or other field trips, she was becoming a total stranger to them. But God somehow added more friends into their life.

Even though Amy lost interest in making new friends and in just being friendly to people, remarkably God brought more happy and positive people into her life outside the church. By December, her son had 16 kids come to his birthday party and only one was from the church. He replaced the lost friends with the new ones. They felt very blessed. She kept reminding herself to Stand on the Promises of Christ her King. As she sang those words she felt God's presence close to her.

STANDING ON THE PROMISES
By Russell Carter

Standing on the promises of Christ my King,
Through eternal ages let His praises ring,
Glory in the highest, I will shout and sing,
Standing on the promises of God.

Standing, standing,
Standing on the promises of God my Savior;
Standing, standing,
I'm standing on the promises of God.

Sometimes as Christians we forget where we stand in life. What is Truth and what isn't? But when Amy was singing this song, it put her feet on firm ground and reminded her of the promises that God has for His children.

AMY WAS REMINDED of the verses in Matthew 23:13-15 and Luke 11:42-53 regarding Woes on the Pharisees and the Experts in the Law.

Matthew 23:13-15 KJV-But woe unto you, scribes and Pharisees, hypocrites! For ye shut up the kingdom of heaven against men: for ye neither go in yourselves, neither suffer ye them that are entering to go in. Woe unto you, scribes and Pharisees, hypocrites! For ye devour widows' houses, and for a pretence make long prayer: therefore ye shall receive the greater damnation. Woe unto you, scribes and Pharisees, hypocrites! For ye compass sea and land to make one proselyte, and when he is made, ye make him twofold more the child of hell than yourselves.

Luke 11:42-53 (NIV) [42] "Woe to you Pharisees, because you give God a tenth of your mint, rue and all other kinds of garden herbs, but you neglect justice and the love of God. You should have practiced the latter without leaving the former undone. [43] "Woe to you Pharisees, because you love the most important seats in the synagogues and respectful greetings in the marketplaces. [44] "Woe to you, because you are like unmarked graves, which people walk over without knowing it." [45] One of the experts in the law answered him, "Teacher, when you say these things, you insult us also." [46] Jesus replied, "And you experts in the law, woe to you, because you load people down with burdens they can hardly carry, and you yourselves will not lift one finger to help them. [47] "Woe to you, because you build tombs for the prophets, and it was your ancestors who killed them. [48] So you testify that you approve of what your ancestors did; they killed the prophets, and you build their tombs. [49] Because of this, God in his wisdom said, 'I will send them prophets and apostles, some of whom they will kill and others they will persecute.' [50] Therefore this generation will be held responsible for the blood of all the prophets that has been shed since the beginning of the world, [51] from the blood of Abel to the blood of Zechariah, who was killed between the altar and the sanctuary. Yes, I tell you, this generation will be held responsible for it all. [52] "Woe to you experts in the law, because you have taken away the key to knowledge. You yourselves have not entered, and you have hindered those who were entering." [53] When Jesus went outside, the

Pharisees and the teachers of the law began to oppose him fiercely and to besiege him with questions,

According to Bibletools.org, "*The real problem with the scribes and Pharisees is that they were totally selfish. They weighted their judgment toward themselves, and so they had no room for mercy for others. Nothing about them resembled Christ—no fidelity. They did not see a need for faith in the forgiveness in Christ, for they felt they needed none.*

Christ gave them the answer to their problem. If they would render proper judgment, without partiality, emphasis on self would diminish. Their mercy would allow people to make mistakes and have space to repent rather than fear being destroyed financially or otherwise. Finally, with true fidelity, they would treat everyone as Christ did. Their faith would increase, as would the faith of those under their influence.

Had they properly applied these three qualities—judgment, mercy, and faith—their attitudes would have turned from selfish carnal goals to outgoing concern for others. They would have begun displaying the real love of God. If we apply them, we will have the confidence and boldness of which Paul spoke—the kind of faith required for salvation. The scribes and Pharisees lacked it. Being alive, we still have the chance to obtain it."

Luke 17:1-3a ¹Jesus said to his disciples: "Things that cause people to stumble are bound to come, but woe to anyone through whom they come. ² It would be better for them to be thrown into the sea with a millstone tied around their neck than to cause one of these little ones to stumble. ³ So watch yourselves...

A MY FOUND PRAYER to be a stress reliever. She'd pray in the daytime while walking with her kids. She'd pray when she woke up in the middle of the night. When troubling thoughts from the meeting flooded into her mind, she had to pray. She lost so much weight that the people that knew her wondered if she was alright. And even though Amy felt overwhelmed by those problems, Bible verses came to mind: *Finally, brethren, whatsoever things are true, whatsoever things are honest, whatsoever things are just, whatsoever things are pure, whatsoever things are lovely, whatsoever things are of good report; if there be any virtue, and if there be any praise, think on these things. Philippians 4:8*

Amy had to think positive thoughts, and thoughtful prayer was positive. God was in control and she had faith in Him though the road was rough. She hung onto God's Word like the verse: *II Corinthians 4:8-9—We are troubled on every side, yet not distressed; we are perplexed, but not in despair; persecuted, but not forsaken; cast down, but not destroyed;*

Truly, God's Word became more powerful and alive in Amy than it had during the 14 years of listening to the sermons of her former pastor. Since she wasn't reading her Bible anymore, the verses in her heart were the only things that kept her afloat. *Psalm 119:11 (KJV) Thy word have I hid in mine heart, that I might not sin against thee.* She was thankful that she learned a lot of verses growing up in Christian School and going to Bible School. Those were her rock in the time of storm.

In the end, Pastor Janus will be held accountable for his actions. It was hard to see him after that and not feel betrayed or disappointed. Praying for him was even harder to do, and yet Amy did.

Even though she still was faithful to His Word he completely stressed her out. She lost a drastic amount of weight and at work she fainted not because of dehydration but because of stress and depression. She lost a lot of work hours and money because she had to stop working for a while. While the Cardio Doctor found nothing wrong with her heart and the Neurologist found nothing wrong with her head, she knew it was the pastor that put this stress on her, a burden so heavy that she struggled to carry it.

JESUS IS THE CENTER OF IT ALL
By Israel Houghton

Jesus at the center of it all
Jesus at the center of it all
From beginning to the end
It will always be, it's always been You Jesus, Jesus.
Nothing else matters, nothing in this world will do
Jesus, You're the center, and everything revolves around You.
Jesus, You at the center of it all.

As she sang the words in this song she realized in her mind that the purpose of her life was to please Jesus Christ and serve Him. She was reminded that the problem was not the center of her life, but Jesus is.

S UMMER CAME; AMY pushed herself to take her son to every Vacation Bible School around their area. Even though she was aching inside, she took him to a total of three different churches that availed it. Amazingly, her son still had his child-like faith. When the teachers asked the kids for volunteers to pray out loud he was one of the first people to enthusiastically raise his hands.

Amy felt bad for her son that they had to switch churches. From birth on up that's where he grew up. Amy prayed that he wasn't affected by the changes that rattled their lives. His prayer partner/godparent was there and all his little buddies. Now he had to make new friends. It was a long adjustment for all of them but through it God taught them to trust in Him. Sadly, at times she found herself spewing out the anger on her children when she recalled the terrible meeting. Amy begged God to take that anger away from her heart. She knew some unsaved people handled problems better than them. But this one left her broken and troubled. It may not have affected their son but it sure did affect her marriage.

A MY'S HUSBAND ARGUED with her, saying, "It is wrong what Pastor Janus is doing, but it's not a sin," even though she talked to a total of 12 different pastors from different states and backgrounds and all agreed that the verse, *"Abstain from the appearance of evil,"* had a universal meaning and was not just for prophecy (adding to the fact that pastors must be blameless at all times). Or else her husband asked, "Who has he hurt?" To him, since this pastor hadn't slept with other women, then it's not a big deal. Amy couldn't understand how a man who had grown up in a Christian home, who went to church every Sunday, who attended Christian College and took Bible Exposition, thought this. His thoughts were far beyond her simple faith and God-fearing mind. A pastor told her, if my wife found out that I was massaging someone she would not be happy and vice versa. Amy told her husband that she was sure the pastor had hurt his wife though they might not know it. When a spouse crossed the line of marriage a trust was broken. One could also feel betrayed and many other feelings that go with that. And it took time to heal.

Mark's words left Amy more bewildered, exhausted and discouraged. Was he just justifying the Truth? He filled their marriage with loose ends. In the end, it was one of those things where they had to agree to disagree. In many marriages, there are challenges. Overall, this tribulation helped Amy and her husband grow closer to each other and to love one other more deeply than when they first met.

As Amy studied a list of the different commentaries of the verse, ı Thessalonians 5:22 Abstain from the appearance of evil, she saw this common denominator: *"Hold yourselves aloof from every evil kind." The word "evil" is used in the moral sense. We should abstain from sin, and whatever looks like sin, leads to it, and borders upon it. He who is not shy of the appearances of sin, who shuns not the occasions of it, and who avoids not the temptations and approaches to it, will not long keep from doing sin,"* said by Matthew Henry Commentary.

"Though there are instances where they cannot be proved to be positively wrong or forbidden, they have much the 'appearance' of evil, and will be so interpreted by others. The safe and proper rule is to lean always to the side of virtue," said Albert Barnes Commentary. And what does the word virtue mean? It means behavior showing high moral standards. The synonyms for virtue are goodness, righteousness, morality, integrity, dignity, honor, respectability, purity, ethics, etc. Were any of these found in Pastor Janus's behavior?

A S FOR THE verse, It is good for a man not to touch a woman. I Corinthians 7:1, to understand its meaning one must read the whole chapter which is about marriage. Below are the commentaries of Matthew Henry, who was a pastor and an author of many Christian books.

"In this chapter the apostle answers some cases proposed to him by the Corinthians about marriage. He shows them that marriage was appointed as a remedy against fornication, and therefore that persons had better marry than burn (v. 1-9). He gives direction to those who are married to continue together, though they might have an unbelieving relative, unless the unbeliever would part, in which case a Christian would not be in bondage (v. 10-16). He shows them that becoming Christians does not change their external

state; and therefore advises everyone to continue, in the general, in that state in which he was called (v. 17-24). He advises them, by reason of the present distress, to keep themselves unmarried; hints the shortness of time, and how they should improve it, so as to grow dead and indifferent to the comforts of the world; and shows them how worldly cares hinder their devotions, and distract them in the service of God (v. 25-35). He directs them in the disposal of their virgins (v. 36-38). And closes the chapter with advice to widows how to dispose of themselves in that state (v. 39, v. 40)."

So, in conclusion, if a couple cannot keep their hands off each other, it is better for them to marry rather than to burn. But if they are married, God commands them to only get a divorce if one has committed fornication. Last, in Amy's opinion, if a married man is not supposed to massage another woman or take single ladies out alone to dinner and places, then how much more does this apply to a man of God? This pastor was definitely not setting a good example. When Amy asked parents how they would have felt if their pastor massaged their daughters many of them responded in horrified anger. "I would never let that happen!" they said. Yet it had happened for years, especially in this church.

Most churches follow a third-party rule. Those in leadership can't be alone with another person other than their husband or wife. There must be a third party at all times, even in the car. They have a logical reason why they follow this rule, both past experience and present.

Also, they have a no PC (personal contact) rule, especially for married individuals, other than shaking hands for greeting. These rules are set up so that they won't fall into temptation. Although in some churches, they find nothing wrong with hugging the opposite sex as long as they have Christ love in their hearts. After all, the Bible talks about treating each other with brotherly love. Would you just shake the hands of your blood brothers or sisters? The answer is likely no. As long as our heart and mind is pure then our family in Christ should be no different. We should treat them like our own blood family.

A CCORDING TO A *Focus on the Family* article Overcoming a Bad Church Experience by David Sanford, *"Approximately 22 million Americans say they are Christians and made a faith commitment to Jesus Christ, and say that commitment is still important to them, but they have struggled with faith or relational issues and therefore quit going to church. Tens of thousands more will join their ranks this week. Like a safe harbor, local churches can be a second home for many people. Sadly, churches also can be the setting for some of the harshest attacks against our faith."* Unfortunately, Amy and her husband Mark became one of the statistics. It was a huge struggle to get back to the spiritual happy life.

Amy always thought that the world would give people problems, but in this case the leaders in the church caused the problems. Ephesians 6:12 (KJV)—For we wrestle not against flesh and blood, but against principalities, against powers, against the rulers of the darkness of this world, against spiritual wickedness in high places.

Songs continuously popped into Amy's mind that encouraged her and kept her from discouragement. She knew it was all God working in her life and was no longer her. She sang so many songs in her darkest days, and she found it amazing when a song she rarely sang somehow came to mind and touched her heart at just the right time.

Qualification of a Pastor

E VENTUALLY, FOUR MONTHS later, Amy Stiles went
online and did research on commentaries from
different Bible teachers, professors and pastors
regarding qualifications of a pastor and unhealthy
churches. It was a way to help her understand the
situation she had gone through. Many of the outlines
had Bible verses which encouraged Amy to begin
reading her Bible again.

The word pastor means shepherd. A shepherd leads,
feeds, comforts, corrects, and protects the sheep under
his care. In fact, a pastor can also be called elder,
overseer and bishop. Amy's eyes were opened as she
read Titus 1:5-9 and 1 Timothy 3:1-7. These two offer
an almost identical list of what the pastor should be
like.

Titus 1:5-9 KJV For this cause left I thee in Crete that thou shouldest set in order the things that are wanting and ordain elders in every city, as I had appointed thee. If <u>any</u> <u>man</u> be <u>blameless, the husband of one wife, having faithful</u> <u>children not accused of riot or unruly</u>. For a bishop must be <u>blameless</u>, as the steward of God not self-willed, <u>not soon</u> <u>angry</u>, <u>not given to wine</u>, <u>no striker</u>, <u>not given to filthy</u> <u>lucre</u>. But a <u>lover of</u> hospitality, a lover of good men, <u>sober,</u> just, holy, <u>temperate;</u> Holding fast the faithful word as he had been taught that he may be able by sound doctrine both to exhort and to convince the gainsayers.

1 Timothy 3:1-7 KJV This is a true saying, if a man <u>desire the office of a bishop</u>, he <u>desireth a good work</u>. A bishop then <u>must be blameless, the husband of one wife</u>, vigilant, <u>sober</u>, of <u>good behavior</u>, <u>given to hospitality</u>, <u>apt to teach</u>. <u>Not</u> <u>given to wine</u>, <u>no striker</u>, <u>not greedy of filthy lucre</u>, but <u>patient</u>, not a <u>brawler</u>, <u>not covetous</u>. One <u>that ruleth well his</u> <u>own house</u>, <u>having his children in subjection with all</u> <u>gravity</u>. (For if a man no not how to rule his own house how shall he take care of the church of God?) <u>Not a novice</u>, lest being lifted up with pride he fall into the condemnations of the devil. Moreover, <u>he must have a good report</u> of them which are without; lest he fall into reproach and the snare of the devil.

The underlined words are explained below by Charles Specht.

BELOW ARE COMMENTARIES from Charles Specht's post, "Twenty Qualification Every Pastor Must

Possess." Specht has served as Senior Pastor of First Baptist Church and as an Associate Pastor in Madera, California. He attended many seminaries and later became a writer and well-known speaker.

"**any man**" – A pastor is to be a man, not a woman ("Let a woman learn in silence with all submission. And I do not permit a woman to teach or to have authority over a man, but to be in silence." 1 Timothy 2:11-12).

"**desires the position**" – Two different Greek words are used to refer to this desire/aspire attitude (the second word is found in #3 below). This first Greek word for "desires" refers to external action and involves pursuing tangible things in order to be found qualified for this office.

"**desires a good work**" – This second Greek word for "desires" refers to the inward motivation/desire a man must have in order to be qualified for this office. He must internally desire the office and not merely be nominated by others for the office.

"**must be blameless**" – The words "must be" are included, stressing the fact that what follows is absolutely necessary. Being "blameless" ("above reproach") literally means "not to be held" in a criminal sense. This is the most important character qualification for the pastor, and the list of qualifications that follow elaborates on what it means to be "blameless." There is to be no unrepentant sin that can be publicly named or pointed to in which the church or civil community is aware of. It doesn't mean he is sinless or has never sinned, but that he can't be held in contempt, either criminally, morally, socially, or ethically.

"husband of one wife" – This literally means to be a "one-woman man". It's not referring to his marital status but to his sexual purity. It doesn't mean he can never have been widowed or be single, for example, but that he is to be solely devoted to one woman if (and while) married. This qualification comes immediately after the necessity of being "blameless" because the area of sexual purity is where many church leaders fail and, thus, become disqualified to serve as pastors.

"temperate" – Literally means to be "wineless," but is here being used metaphorically and means to be "alert" or "watchful" or "clear-headed." The pastor needs to have a "good head" on his shoulders and be watchful for things that might creep into his congregation, such as sexual sin, heresy, or false teachers.

"sober-minded" – He is to be a serious man who knows how to order his priorities.

"of good behavior" – Means to be "orderly"…as opposed to being chaotic or disorganized.

"hospitable" – Means to have a "love of strangers." The pastor must set the example about how to be open and available for others, always being ready to be social and receptive of Christians and non-Christians alike.

"able to teach" – The only qualification referring to the pastor's spiritual giftedness/ability, and the only one that distinguishes the office of pastor from that of deacon. Preaching and teaching God's Holy Word is the primary responsibility of the pastor in the local church.

"not given to wine" – Not a regular drinker of alcohol. The pastor must never consume alcohol because he could be called on at any time of the day or night to perform his duties and, therefore, his judgment must never be clouded by alcohol.

"not violent" – Literally, "not a giver of blows." A pastor is to be a humble, patient man who is calm and gentle and doesn't react with physical violence.

"not greedy for money" – He is not in the ministry to make money, and earning money is not his motivation for ministry or service. The stress is on not being "greedy," so the pastor is not to be concerned about money since the Lord will take care of his daily needs.

"gentle" – Means to be gracious, quick to forgive; Does not hold a grudge.

"not quarrelsome" – Seeks for peace; Reluctant to fight or argue.

"**not covetous**" – The pastor's desire is to be for the love of God and His people, not for the love of money, possessions or position. A covetous man demonstrates a lifestyle/attitude that is not blameless.

"**one who rules his own house well**" – The pastor's home life (as well as his personal life) must be well-ordered, not chaotic. This refers to his relationship with his wife, any children, and all things connected with his home life. A divorced man shows no sign of ruling his own home well and, therefore, would not qualify to be a pastor.

"**having his children in submission with all reverence**" – A pastor must have the respect of his children and they must be well-behaved. This does not mean that a man must have children in order to be a pastor, but if he does have any children then they must be submissive to him and his authority over them.

"**not a novice**" – Not a new convert. A newly converted Christian is not mature in the faith and his spiritual leadership would be inadequate, resulting in a prideful, destructive ministry. Pastors are to be spiritually mature, possessing a solid understanding and proper application of the Scriptures.

"**must have a good testimony among those who are outside**" – A pastor must have a good reputation with the surrounding community he lives and ministers in, particularly when it comes to unbelievers. Although non-Christians may disagree with his morals or spiritual beliefs, he must be respected as an honest, caring person (good testimony).

THESE QUALIFICATIONS HAVE been the same for almost 2,000 years. Jesus is the perfect fulfillment of these qualifications as the "senior pastor" of the church. So, if pastors were to follow Christ as the perfect example they should also apply these commands to their lives. Matthew 23:11-12 But he that is greatest among you shall be your servant. And whosoever shall exalt himself shall be abased; and he that shall humble himself shall be exalted. By God's design, leadership in the church is a position of humility and selflessness.

However, in today's society the name Pastor has merely become a title instead of the biblical meaning. Pastors come to church wearing the best suit and tie but never do anything like pick up trash off the floor and beside teaching and preaching. To be a pastor is to be a servant. A servant so loving that he would give up his life for his flock. John 10:15 KJV says, "...and I lay down my life for the sheep. The under shepherd is to reflect the Shepherd which is Christ-- a love so strong that He made Himself a sinner for us so that we could go to heaven. Despite being rejected and shamed he willingly took up the cup and said, "Not my will but thine." Pastors are to reflect a God who cares and points his congregation to the Savior.

GLENN DAMAN, A pastor with two masters degrees from Western Seminary and a Doctor of Ministry from Trinity Evangelical Divinity School, pastors at Stevenson First Baptist Church in the state of Washington. In his book, *When Sheep Squabble-Dealing with Conflict in the* Smaller *Church*, Pastor Daman says, *"Conflict is a reality in every church, whether it is large or small. The task of pastoral leadership is not to eradicate every conflict in the church, but to help people resolve the conflicts in a way that honors Christ, protects the people, and manifests love within the congregation. To achieve this, the pastor of a small church must be proactive in conflict resolution. Too often, pastors assume that love will override the conflict because a small church is relationally driven and enjoys close interpersonal relationships. This is often not the case.*

Unresolved conflict becomes the seedbed of dissension and division and can destroy the closeness of the church and undermine its ministry. Pastors need to be active in assisting people to communicate openly and honestly about disagreements and to work toward mutually agreeable solutions.

When the pastor and the board become involved in the resolution, the effects of the tension on the whole congregation will be minimized. When the congregation knows the board is united, they are more willing to remain on the sidelines rather than become involved in the dispute. Furthermore, when they see the issue being resolved by the board, they are less likely to become stressed by the crisis. Instead, they will remain confident that God is at work in the church.

Moreover, when pastors resolve conflict in a godly manner and communicate clearly with the board, they maintain a spiritually healthy and vibrant church even in the midst of disagreements. Conflict does not need to destroy the ministry of the pastor or the church. It can become a springboard for spiritual growth as people learn to communicate clearly, love unconditionally, and forgive completely. It is not the absence of conflict that distinguishes a loving church, but the resolution of it. When pastors successfully resolve conflict within the church, it distinguishes the church from an unloving world where bitterness, anger, and hostilities destroy relationships. When the people in the church love their enemies, accept one another in spite of their differences, and resolve their disagreements, then all men will know that they are Christ's disciples from the love they have for one another (John 13:35).

The church that does not deal with sin among the members will open the door to more problems. The church is not called to be judgmental of unbelievers, but the church is expected to confront and restore believers who are unrepentant of sins such as those listed in 1 Corinthians 5:11: " . . . anyone who calls himself a brother but is sexually immoral or greedy, an idolater or a slanderer, a drunkard or a swindler." Such individuals are to not be accepted by the church until they are willing to repent. Matthew 18:15-17 provides a concise procedure for the confrontation and restoration of a believer. Matthew 18:15-17 (KJV)—[15] Moreover if thy brother shall trespass against thee, go and tell him his fault between thee and him alone: if he shall hear thee, thou hast gained thy brother. [16] But if he will not hear thee, then take with thee one or two more, that in the mouth of two or three witnesses every word may be established. [17] And if he shall neglect to hear them, tell it unto the church: but if he neglect to hear the church, let him be unto thee as an heathen man and a publican.

Confrontation should be done carefully, meekly, and with the goal of restoration (Galatians 6:1). Churches that lovingly discipline sinning individuals will curtail a great deal of conflict in the church. Galatians 6:1 (KJV) Brethren, if a man be overtaken in a fault, ye which are spiritual, restore such a one in the spirit of meekness; considering thyself, lest thou also be tempted.

At times believers might not be content with the direction or actions of church leaders. This was the case early in the history of the church (Acts 6:1-7). Complaints about the lack of care of a certain group in the church were taken up with the leaders. This was remedied, and the church grew (Acts 6:7). The early church used a conflict to improve the ministry. However, when churches do not have a clear process for dealing with such concerns, people tend to create their own platforms. Individuals may begin polling others in the church, get involved in gossip, or even develop a bloc of "concerned people."

And that's what happened in Pastor Janus's church. The pastor had no interest in apologizing to the church for his secret sin, so it became a rumor, then gossip, and soon groups of people had this in the back of their minds. Do you think they were able to grow spiritually mature? Amy can honestly say no because the leaders were not setting a good example.

Sometimes it is advisable that churches should have two pastors: One senior and one assistant pastor. Having accountability and a mentor can help their church grow strong. With this, the pastor can avoid abuse of power, temptations, dictatorship, etc.

Amy will admit that this pastor that she is writing about has done good things for other people. He could be generous and was also kind when he wanted to be. But at the same time, this pastor has done many unethical things and has violated numerous qualifications of a pastor. He uses religion to make himself look good and to get what he wants.

THROUGHOUT HER CHRISTIAN life Amy had seen several pastors who chose to live a selfish life rather than to do what was right. Ten years ago, a young pastor with his quiet family seemed to lead a peaceful, small church in Pennsylvania. Years later, however, the police arrested the pastor for taking naked pictures of himself and sending them to teenage girls. What a shock that was considering he had two young daughters of his own! He went through a preliminary hearing and was charged with two counts of corruption of minors, and a misdemeanor. Now he no longer preaches.

Then three years after that, while Amy lived in New York, a church was sending an older couple as missionaries overseas. Their desire to be missionaries was evident in their home church. The husband preached many times and attended Bible School. They also were very active in numerous ministries in the church. They already had three, grown, married kids with several grandchildren. All of the sudden, though, the news broke that the husband had been having an affair with another young man overseas. Their home church halted the mission work. Apparently, he wasn't thinking of the consequences. This pastor was dismissed from pastoral positions and now his family doesn't even live with him anymore.

In Amy's opinion, a situation like this made it very hard to trust churches and people again and even read the Bible. It was very heart-breaking for her, almost unreal. When Amy asked over 50 people – both Christian and non-Christian – if a pastor should massage and take ladies out the answer was overwhelmingly negative. Even the atheists disagreed with his behavior.

She felt the meeting with Pastor Janus should have been brought up to the congregation instead of just to the deacons. Then he should have sincerely apologized to the church and to Amy. Moreover, he should have stepped down and sought help through counseling. In the future, he could be restored if the congregation agreed. If the church found nothing wrong with his action, then it was an unhealthy church. It's the leader's fault and hopefully one day their eyes would be opened. In the meantime, she'd just go to a different church. There were no perfect people but to be a pastor he had be holy, blameless and set an example to follow. He needed to realize that he had a higher calling above everyone.

K EEP IN MIND that not all pastors are two-faced. Last February 2018 Billy Graham died. According to the newspaper he left a great legacy quoting: "His reputation was untouched by sex or financial scandal." What a great way to leave the world knowing you've set a superior example and have made our Heavenly Father proud.

Amy remembered her pastor in her Lancaster, Pennsylvania hometown, how he was not only a pastor but how he was also a handyman. He constantly fixed things in the church/school like the swimming pool, vacuum, lights, etc. The only time he was in his suit and tie was when he was preaching. He never traveled anywhere overseas but rooted himself in that church day after day until he died. He built that church with his own bare hands. Some considered him a cheap person, but he was wise in using God's money.

There are many other great pastors that we can learn from such as Billy Sunday, D.L. Moody or even pastors at your own home church. Praise God for those who willingly give their time and lives for Christ. May we not forget their deeds and sacrifice. II Samuel 23:3&4 The Rock of Israel has said to me: when one rules justly over men, ruling in the fear of God, He dawns on them like the morning light, like the sun shining forth on the cloudless morning, like a rain that makes grass to sprout from the earth.

Pulpit's Commentary on the above verse: A king who rules his people justly is as glorious as the sun rising in its strength to drive away the works of darkness, and give men, by precept and example, the light of clear knowledge of their duty.

Qualification of a Deacon

AMY STILES ALSO studied about the qualifications of deacons. Deacon means a servant, a transliteration of the Greek word for "table servant" or "waiter." 1 Timothy 3:8-16 expounds on the qualifications for the office of deacons. 1 Timothy 3:8-16 KJV-Likewise must the deacons be grave, not doubletongued, not given to much wine, not greedy of filthy lucre; Holding the mystery of the faith in a pure conscience. And let these also first be proved; then let them use the office of a deacon, being found blameless. Even so must their wives be grave, not slanderers, sober, faithful in all things. Let the deacons be the husbands of one wife, ruling their children and their own houses well. For they that have used the office of a deacon well purchase to themselves a good degree, and great boldness in the faith which is in Christ Jesus. These things write I unto thee, hoping to come unto thee shortly: But if I tarry long, that thou mayest know how thou oughtest to behave thyself in the house of God, which is the church of the living God, the pillar and ground of the Truth. And without controversy great is the mystery of godliness: God was manifest in the flesh, justified in the Spirit, seen of angels, preached unto the Gentiles, believed on in the world, received up into glory.

Below is the exposition from Dr. Jerry Hullinger on 1 Timothy 3:8-16. Dr. Jerry Hullinger completed his theological training at the historical, evangelical institutions of Moody Bible Institute and Dallas Theological Seminary. Upon graduation he served as a pastor and then as a college/seminary professor and came to Piedmont International University in the fall of 2009. These spiritual qualifications for deacons are explain in detail so the deacons may know how to behave and live.

"Grave" vs.8-a person of dignity, worthy of respect

"Not double-tongue" vs.8-he is not two-faced, not hypocritical, he is sincere.

"Not given to much wine" vs.8-he must not use wine unwisely in any way, nor be enslaved by it or any other food or drink that impairs his judgment.

"Not greedy or filthy lucre" vs.8- He is not in the ministry to make money and earning money is not his motivation for ministry or service. The stress is on not being "greedy," so the deacon is not to be concerned money since the Lord will take care of his daily needs.

"Holding the faith...with pure conscience" vs.9-describes a man whose convictions and beliefs are consistent with his behavior and it refers to the body of doctrine which had come through special revelation.

"And let these also first be proved" vs.10-two things it does not mean: not referring to an ordination exam and not meaning that a deacon should be given a trial. The Point: the church leaders should constantly be examining the members of the congregation (which is part of their oversight duties) and when the need for deacon arises they will be aware of who would be a good choice. This is the norm resp. for our oversight.

"Blameless" vs.10-no reasonable ground for accusation.

"Even so must their wives be grave" vs.11-dignified, worthy of respect.

"Not be slanderers" vs.11-not gossipers, not wordy; Here particularly emphasizes the slandering aspect.

"Sober" vs.11-well balanced, temperate

"Faithful in all things" vs.11-completely trustworthy.

"Let the deacons be the husband of one wife" vs.12-This requirement means that if a man is married, he must not have two wives. This is an express prohibition of polygamy for a deacon.

"Ruling their children" vs.12-He is the spiritual leader of his home.

"Purchases to himself a good degree" vs.13-if he serves well as a deacon, he will have good reputation.

"Great boldness in the faith" vs.13-he will have confidence in the things of God, in dealing with people.

In conclusion, the deacons have standards that are set very high because the servant-work of a deacon is a high-profile ministry that requires spiritual maturity, and the qualifications especially stress honesty and family life. Even though the qualifications are high, they are not as high as those for elders because more is required of those who would serve in the highest levels of leadership.

Acts 6:1-8 KJV-And in those days, when the number of the disciples was multiplied, there arose a murmuring of the Grecians against the Hebrews, because their widows were neglected in the daily ministration. Then the twelve called the multitude of the disciples unto them, and said, It is not reason that we should leave the word of God, and serve tables. Wherefore, brethren, look ye out among you seven men of honest report, full of the Holy Ghost and wisdom, whom we may appoint over this business. But we will give ourselves continually to prayer, and to the ministry of the word. And the saying pleased the whole multitude: and they chose Stephen, a man full of faith and of the Holy Ghost, and Philip, and Prochorus, and Nicanor, and Timon, and Parmenas, and Nicolas a proselyte of Antioch: Whom they set before the apostles: and when they had prayed, they laid their hands on them. And the word of

God increased; and the number of the disciples multiplied in Jerusalem greatly; and a great company of the priests were obedient to the faith. And Stephen, full of faith and power, did great wonders and miracles among the people.

These verses are explained by Derek Gentle in, "A Study in the Biblical Role of Deacons." Gentle is a pastor in Birmingham, Alabama, where he has led for almost 20 years. He is a graduate of Southwestern Baptist Theological Seminary in Fort Worth. He says,

The Office of Deacon Was Created for the Purpose of Handling the Benevolence Ministry—The Biblical account is quite clear on the founding of the deaconship and nowhere does Scripture repeal the original purpose: Acts 6:1-3 (KJV) And in those days, when the number of the disciples was multiplied, there arose a murmuring of the Grecians against the Hebrews, because their widows were neglected in the daily ministration. Then the twelve called the multitude of the disciples unto them, and said, It is not reason that we should leave the word of God, and serve tables. Wherefore, brethren, look ye out among you seven men of honest report, full of the Holy Ghost and wisdom, whom we may appoint over this business.

The Office of Deacon Was Established to Free the Apostles (who functioned as the first pastors) to Pray and to Prepare to Minister the Word—The Apostles, in dealing with the benevolence ministry problem at the Jerusalem church, told the congregation that, "It is not

desirable that we should leave the word of God and serve tables. Therefore, brethren, seek out from among you seven men of good reputation, full of the Holy Spirit and wisdom, whom we may appoint over this business; but we will give ourselves continually to prayer and to the ministry of the word." Acts 6:2-4 (NKJV) Some have understood this passage to mean that it is the role of deacons to oversee the business of the church. First, the text says, "this business," not "the business" — and the business being referred to is the business of benevolence. Second, as Dr. Robert Naylor points out, that would be a misrepresentation of the meaning of the word: "The word 'business' should be discussed a little to prevent any misunderstanding. The Greek word is chreia and basically means 'need.' It is so translated 25 times. This is the only place it is translated 'business.' Hence there is no Scriptural authority for the deacons to make financial decisions of the church. Church decisions must remain church decisions."

The Early Deacons Were Selected for Their Spiritual Qualifications—*1st Timothy 3 and Acts 6 expound the qualifications for the office of deacons; the later contains what could fairly be called the "core qualifications": "Men of good reputation, full of the Holy Spirit and wisdom" — Acts 6:3 "And they chose Stephen, a man full of faith and the Holy Spirit" — Acts 6:5 Often, when someone is discussed as a possible deacon one hears a remark such as, "He attends regularly and is a good giver." But God is looking at men with an internal* dynamic, which cannot be determined in a superficial way.

Deacons Are to Be Capable of Serving the Lord in Spiritual Ways—The original seven deacons were people who were able to serve the Lord in ways which were more spiritual in nature than merely delivering food. Stephen was a man of spiritual power: "And Stephen, full of faith and power, did great wonders and signs among the people" (Acts 6:8 NJKV). Philip was not only a deacon, but also was gifted in evangelism (Acts 8:5-7).

The Office of Deacon Requires a Firm Grasp of Sound Doctrine—A church is content oriented. It is a doctrinally driven community, built upon Truth. Every member should have this approach in this fellowship; leaders such as deacons, not less but, more so. "They must possess the mystic secret of the faith [Christian Truth as hidden from ungodly men] with a clear conscience" Acts 6:9 (Amplified)

The Presence of Deacons Should Advance the Unity of a Church—When the Apostles laid out the plan for the creation of this office, "The saying pleased the whole multitude" (Acts 6:5 NKJV). The complaints about the benevolence ministry stopped. And the complaints were by the Greek speaking Jews, the Hebrew speaking Jews obviously bent over backwards to preserve the church's unity, for all the men selected had Greek names. It is still true today: Any time a church has deacons who are *properly doing their jobs, the church is more likely to be at unity.*

***The Presence of Deacons Should Advance the Cause of Evangelism**—The immediate impact of the creation of the office of deacon was to eliminate the controversy in the church and to get the church back on course in fulfilling its mission. The Bible says that, "Then the word of God spread, and the number of the disciples multiplied greatly in Jerusalem, and a great many of the priests were obedient to the faith" (Acts 6:8 NKJV). Again, it is still true. When a church has deacons who are in God's will, the cause of world evangelization will be aided.*

I T WAS VERY disheartening to know that many deacons serving in the church protected the reputation of the pastor instead of doing what was right. Amy met many of these deacons in this church and treated them as her father and/or her brother in the Lord. Many times, though, she questioned their character and spiritual growth. Even so, the pastor and some members seemed to have no problem qualifying them as deacons.

Even in a Catholic church, reputation is very important. Why do you think many of the priests that have molested and raped both boys and girls have not been sent to jail? It goes back to the word "reputation." They don't want the church to get sued so they cover up sin. They don't want to lose their congregation, they don't want to have a bad name, they don't want to lose financially, etc. And so, instead of enforcing justice, they just move their priest around, either to different states or countries.

Although, there is a difference between a Catholic church and a Christian Evangelical church leadership; For example, the Catholic Church has one leader which is the Pope. They are all connected to one another like an institution. But the Christian Evangelical church is under different pastors. Each church has different leaders. In an Evangelical church (meaning according to the teaching of the gospel, scriptural, biblical and fundamentalist) when a pastor or deacon has committed a sin, they are dismissed from their position and, if it's a hideous crime, they are sent to jail. The church may close down, or a new pastor takes over.

Too much control of the deacons or pastors and priest can make a church spiritually and morally crumble rather than build it up in God's glory. God wants believers to work together as a family of God rather than to dictate. Many times, deacons don't speak up or say something against the pastor because they carry a burden of betrayal. Since the pastor has done them a favor they feel they must honor him. To tell on the pastor would be considered a 'snitch.' He might counter back by revealing their secret sinful lives also. So, it is best to repent and do right from the start.

After Amy and her family left the church, the brave deacon that stood up for her at the meeting decided to follow God's call to be a Chaplain in the United States Army. So, they left the church and the deacon that they replaced him with was a man who owed Amy and Mark

$400.00 from eight years ago. As you can tell, the church ignored these leaders' minimal degree of conviction, and their low standard qualifications. If they were true believers in Christ, they would take God's commands seriously.

Church Searching

LEAVING THAT PARTICULAR church under bad circumstances tempted Amy and Mark to abandon church entirely. Amy Stiles felt that Pastor Janus should have been the one to leave instead of them. Situations like this should never happen at all in a Bible believing church.

It was very difficult to find the right church. Even the churches that her friends took her to were not what she expected. It was a very disappointing and discouraging experience. Amy had to force herself to look for a church where she and her children could grow spiritually and enjoy it.

They first went to Fellowship Baptist Church, which was mostly comprised of African American people. At this time, Amy did not care what was the nationality make-up of the church she attended as long as it was not like the first church. Fellowship Baptist had a great charismatic and devoted pastor that could preach from the heart. He was friendly and so were the people. Both worship and church services were moving; They kept everyone awake. She always heard an outburst of "Amen" and applause.

Their music was both in modern and traditional hymnal songs. And they had more than just piano or drums for instruments. Amy loved all the lively music that they played. However, during the sermon the children were in the sanctuary, bored to death, and getting on their mother's nerves. Since there was no Sunday School for the children they caused distraction, not only to their mothers but also to the people around them. Mothers wanted to worship and grow spiritually too but how could they when there was no Nursery? There was no Bible Study during the weekdays, either, so they only gathered on Sunday morning, no evening service available. Amy wanted to volunteer to teach Sunday School, but with two young kids on her hands it was impossible. She knew she needed to be spiritually mended and most importantly healed from her traumatic experience. She felt God wanted her to move on.

THE SECOND CHURCH they visited was similar to the Asian church where they used to attend. It was very family oriented. Everyone called each other

Aunties and Uncles, brother or sister and Lolo and Lola. They kept that part of the tradition too. The worship songs were mostly in modern songs with instruments like drums, electric guitars and tambourines. Children's choir did some dancing and hand motion. There was no dress code required. They had Bible studies every Friday night with refreshment at the end.

The pastor was friendly and nice. His sermon was simple and down to earth. After church services they had a free lunch for everyone. Fellowshipping was very important, and it could last for hours. They allowed kids to have birthday parties where everyone joined in. Anniversaries, weddings and baby showers were frequent too.

Amy's husband did not like the pastor there since he was close to his godfather and they were best friends. As for her son, he had difficulty blending with the children since most of them were related. So, as a caring wife and mother, Amy mainly left the church to appease the family.

FINALLY, THE THIRD church was a traditional Baptist church. They had two pastors. Both men were great pastors whose sermons were not just milk of the Word of God but meat to chew all week. The children had their own Sunday School in the morning and afterwards they'd sit quietly in church for morning service with their parents. I think this arrangement taught children to behave and sit still rather than to just run around and play all the time. They had children's choir but were not allowed to do any motion or dance. They had to remain still. Dress code was definitely enforced, especially when it came to singing up front. The only instruments they had were an organ, piano and a trumpet.

The leaders were highly respected but with cordiality. This was the type of church in which Amy had grown up in Pennsylvania—very conservative. Amy's son enjoyed going there too and accepted Jesus in his heart a year later. He loves his Sunday School teacher and other children's ministries like Boys and Girls for Jesus during the winter and Vacation Bible School during the summer.

Her husband, Mark, liked the preaching there. He knew these pastors were very knowledgeable about the Bible from the way they preached. As for Amy she loved the fact that they had a nursery for her one-year-old daughter and what a relief for Amy! She was able to relax and listen to the sermon and mingle a little to get to know some people. There was no fellowship after the church service where you could sit down, eat and talk with other people, but small snacks were given. Those were the things Amy did miss; Most of the time after church service they'd go to a restaurant. Nevertheless, it was their home church for now.

Amy also noticed that the pastors were very concerned for their congregation's spiritual growth, because they always had Our Daily Bread and other free devotional booklets available plus tracks galore at the main entrance every Sunday for all to give out or keep. This validated where the leaders' hearts were. Amy hoped and prayed deeply that this was the church God wanted them to stay at permanently after several months of searching.

Amy wanted her children to experience the fun and loving church that she once had—a church that they could call their second home. But a church that is based on tradition, man-made rules, and leaders that are dictators should instead cause alarm. On the other hand, she was thankful that they were out of their old church. In their new church they could now actually listen to the preacher and not dwell on the sin the pastor committed. The respect she had for her new pastors was not rooted in fear but rather in legitimate esteem, humility and gratitude.

BALANCED CHRISTIAN LIFE

A MY THOUGHT THAT we, at times, forgot to live a balanced Christian life. As leaders we made rules or followed rules that were too extreme or had no rules at all. Amy loved the article by Steve Arterburn, the founder of the Women of Faith conferences and New Life Ministries. This article is based on his book, ***More Jesus, Less Religion***, from WaterBrook Press.

Growing up in a church that had many written and unwritten rules was not a positive experience. To me, each rule presented a challenge: Either figure out a way around it or live without it. I could not relate to a faith experience that was dictated by a group of male rule-makers and the rules they established. Some of the rules were understandable—such as not drinking or smoking. As an adolescent, I had no business doing either.

The problem came when the rules became more important than relationships. Our family took rule-following to the extreme, and it affected all our relationships. Rules that focus on a minor area of life can come to take precedence over the greater priorities of building character and connecting relationally. Why? Rather than creating a heart that is good, following a rule is something that makes the church and the family look good.

Modern-day legalists act just like the Pharisees in the days of Christ. They are so caught up in the traditions and rigid rules of their own kingdoms they fail to see that mercy and grace are just as important as discipline and sacrifice (Hos. 6:6). Love, not legalism, must reign. Then when a Spirit-filled connection is formed, even between people with different traditions or theologies, respect flows from the heart and changes attitudes and behaviors. Jesus had a way of walking right into the midst of the rejected and the untouchables and drawing them to Him. He still does it today when we give first place to the law of love and allow His Truth to pour out from our hearts and our hands. When we commit ourselves to having more Jesus and less of our ruthless religion, we feel His love and respectfully share it with those who are of no less importance to Him than we are.

After attending so many churches, sadly, she had seen churches where the kids were not allowed to be kids, where they were yelled at for running around when there were no sermons. They would say this is God's house but that is not true! A church is just a building. What makes it a church are God's people. We are the body of Christ. We are the church.

Some also made rules like when kids were not allowed to sing in the Kids Choir because they were not wearing ties. Where is that found in the Bible? Some church leaders expected the children to sit still for hours when they couldn't even do that themselves. The church doesn't realize that if they don't accept the children, the mothers will not feel welcome or accepted either. Didn't Jesus himself say, "Let the little children come unto me?"

Amy had been to churches where they were more concerned about crumbs getting on the carpet due to mothers feeding their hungry children during long services than they were concerned for the people. Recently in the news, there was severe flooding due to a hurricane in Houston, Texas. The press criticized a popular pastor for not letting displaced people in his mega church. It seemed to Amy he was more concerned about damage done to the church building than helping people who were suffering. As Christians, we must remember that our ministry is people. We must show the same likeness of love that Christ did for us.

Amy had also been to churches where they didn't allow their young adults who were part of a choir or other church leadership to date. To date, as in going out as boyfriend and girlfriend. The pastor said, "No dating allowed until both get a professional job." Where is that found in the Bible? Love was created by God and how can church leaders stop their feelings for one another when it is so natural? Instead the pastor became a parent to these young adults rather than a friend. A pastor's job is to help his congregation to grow spiritually mature rather than to act as a dictator. No wonder many are leaving the church. Most of the rules are man-made and are so overwhelming that even they themselves and their families can't even follow many of their extreme rules.

With these unbiblical and unloving man-made rules Amy believed we have characterized Christ to the unbelievers and to growing Christians as an angry and unmerciful God who burdens people with weights that even they themselves cannot carry. But to the innocent poor children they know intuitively that Jesus is not like that. To them, Jesus is gentle, caring, loving and forgiving.

SPIRITUAL GIFTS

WE MAY BE many but each of us has different and important God given spiritual gifts and talents. I Corinthians 12:4-27 KJV-Now there are diversities of gifts, but the same Spirit. And there are differences of administrations, but the same Lord. And there are diversities of operations, but it is the same God which worketh all in all. But the manifestation of the Spirit is given to every man to profit withal. For to one is given by the Spirit the word of wisdom; to another the word of knowledge by the same Spirit; To another faith by the same Spirit; to another the gifts of healing by the same Spirit; To another the working of miracles; to another prophecy; to another discerning of spirits; to another divers kinds of tongues; to another the interpretation of tongues: But all these worketh that one and the selfsame Spirit, dividing to every man severally as he will. For as the body is one, and hath many members, and all the members of that one body, being many, are one body: so also is Christ.

While some are called to be missionaries, some as teachers we must all learn to get along no matter what our spiritual gifts are, color and even beliefs. There must be unity in our gathering for we are all a family of Christ. So, when church members leave due to a quarrel there will be hurt, an open wound, and a cut that can never be healed because the body of Christ has been severed. God does not like to see that happening. It affects the whole body unless something godly is done rather than wounding the spirit.

Amy remembered a fun children's song called THE BODY OF CHRIST. This is how it goes:

Chorus 1
We are the body of Christ 2X
Together bringing His love to the world
We work together 2X
We do it with cooperation
We work together 2X
We do it with cooperation
Amen

Verse 1
I am the eye I go blink blink
Yes I am the eye and I can wink
I am the eye but I can't think
That belongs to my friend the brain

Verse 2
I fritter fratter frit. Fritter fratter frit
I'm the brain with electric current patter pit
I'm the brain and I fritter. Learning bit by bit
Yes I fritter fratter fritter all the time

Verse 3
I go lub dub. Lub dub I go
I am the heart. I pump like so
I'm bringing life to all the parts
I am consistent I'm the heart

Verse 4
I'm swinging I'm swinging
Swinging on life's merry way
I'm the arm, I'm the arm
I'm bringing grace to all

Verse 5
Hearing, hearing
Small ears hearing
We don't miss much
Hearing all the time

This is a very fun song making it easy for the children to remember. It teaches the church kids that we are all a family of Christ though we are many and all different; We must work, respect each other and get along bringing His love to the world.

SHOULD PASTORS HAVE ANOTHER JOB?

THERE IS NOTHING wrong with pastors having a job. As a matter of fact, apostle Paul himself had a job as a tent maker while preaching full time. He refused to be paid by the church believing he would rather teach out of love rather than for profit. He displayed a certain pride in his hardworking lifestyle. In 1 Thessalonians 2:9 (KJV) For ye remember, brethren, our labour and travail: for labouring night and day, because we would not be chargeable unto any of you, we preached unto you the gospel of God. He didn't want to be a financial burden to those he ministered to. His hands were most likely calloused due to his continuous tent making skill.

He also did this to set an example of diligence. In 2 Thessalonians 3:7-8 Paul says, For yourselves know how ye ought to follow us: for we behaved not ourselves disorderly among you. He didn't make money his priority, but he emphasized work ethic. Laziness was definitely not in his character. He worked hard so he can help the weak and the poor. That's why he said, It is better to give than to receive.

Some churches do encourage pastors to have a job so they don't depend on the church so much for everything. Even missionaries sometimes are likely to take advantage of the benefits. Soon they have someone doing their laundry, cleaning their house for a cheap labor.

If they are to work, makes sure it's a job that doesn't cross the line of qualification for a pastor or deacons. We are here on this earth to glorify God. The bible says, Whether therefore ye eat, or drink, or whatsoever ye do, do all to the glory of God. 1 Corinthians 10:31 (KJV)

RELIGION VS. FAITH

THE WAY TO be right with God in every religion is by earning your way. It is based on works, not grace. Christianity, on the other hand, is different from every religion in this respect: all other religions (including Mormonism, Islam, Hinduism, and Buddhism) state that you must earn the right to reconcile with God. What you do in this life (good deeds or bad deeds) determines your eternal destiny. Christianity is completely different from this. It is not religion.

There is a big difference between Religion and Faith. Religion is man trying to reach up to God. The message of Christianity is God reaching down to man. Religion is about what man has to do to be right with God. Christianity is about what God has already done to provide us the opportunity to be right with Him. Religion says you must earn your salvation by doing good deeds or certain acts and avoiding evil. Christianity says all we need to do is believe that Christ has already paid the price for the evil we have done. Religion says we are all evil (filled with sin) and there is nothing we can do to earn the right to be saved. Christianity says that God (in the form of Jesus Christ) stepped into our place and paid the awful price that had to be paid for us. He gave us the free gift of Salvation if we choose to believe in Jesus. This is the difference between religion and true Christianity. There is no checklist or list of rules that you must follow. It is all about your relationships, vertical and horizontal. There is no rhetoric or rituals that have to be practiced. Believe that Jesus Christ came to earth and died for your sins, accept his FREE GIFT, let God help you to love Him and love others. That's it! It is so simple it sounds stupid, and it would be if there was no real power here. I'm here to testify that when you do this, the relationship with God is REAL and the power to change your life is there! Religion is empty. But, in Christ there is power.

So, when you look around at the church and what has happened in history you see a lot of bad things, and some good as well. The key thing that you must understand is that historically "the church" is predominately a religious organization with man-made rules and controls. This is evil, and God is not in it. Good has been done by the few that truly understand what it means to be a Christian. These look like Christ. The Bible says, "You will know them by their fruits." 1 John 2:5-6 -But whoso keepeth his word, in him verily is the love of God perfected: hereby know we that we are in him. He that saith he abideth in him ought himself also so to walk, even as he walked.

This article is written by Jake McWhirter, a captain in the US Air Force and a lover of God.

When we work together we have one vision, one goal, one spirit and one heart. John 13:35 — By this shall all [men] know that ye are my disciples, if ye have love one to another. 1 Corinthians 13:13 — And now abideth faith, hope, charity, these three; but the greatest of these [is] charity. The Bible's main topic is about love. Agape love that is selfless, sacrificial, unconditional love which is what Jesus did on the cross. The word "love" appears 310 times in the King James Bible more than the word hate. Love should be our theme in our home church not rules or dictatorship. For God's love is our Salvation. He loves us so much despite our sinful past and nature. He has removed our transgression as far as the East is from the West. *John 3:16* clearly says, *For God so loved the world that He gave His only begotten Son that whosoever believeth in Him should not perish but have everlasting life.*

Have you as a reader accepted Jesus in your heart? God loves you very much. All you have to do is accept Him into your heart, believe on the Lord Jesus Christ and confess your sins to Him. God made it so easy for us to be His adopted children and heirs of His Kingdom. Turn from your wicked ways and come to Him now. If you have done that you now have eternal life when you die. You don't need to be fearful of death. For the Bible says, *1 Corinthians 15:55-57 O death, where is thy sting? O grave, where is thy victory? The sting of death is sin; and the strength of sin is the law. But thanks be to God, which giveth us the victory through our Lord Jesus Christ.* While living on this earth you must now grow spiritually by reading your Bible and praying every day that is how we grow. Then the Holy Spirit will fill you *Galatians 5:22-23 But the fruit of the Spirit is love, joy, peace, longsuffering, gentleness, goodness, faith, meekness, temperance: against such there is no law.* You are now a new man/woman with a new character, a child of God, forgiven, redeemed and deeply loved! This is grace for you. Despite how sinful we were Grace has made it possible to come to God because of Jesus Christ dying on the cross for our sin. As the song goes, *Amazing grace how sweet that sound that saved a wretch like me. I was once lost but now I'm found was blind but now I see.*

When we have God's love as the Bible says, it will cover a multitude of sins. There will be less quarreling, less selfish acts but humbleness and peace. In 1 John 4:7-8 (KJV) Every one that loveth is born of God, and knoweth God.⁸ He that loveth not knoweth not God; for God is love. Was there any love the way this pastor handled this meeting? No, especially when he made threats to take people to court. He's no different from the world.

BIBLE IS USED FOR REPROOF & REBUKE

THE BIBLE IS not only used to preach but also used to reprove and rebuke. Some people have a hard time taking rebuke or correction from other people. Amy guessed since some of these pastors think they know it all, it crushes their pride and/or ego when they are corrected. In the end, they are only hurting themselves. Revelation 3:19-Those whom I love, I reprove and discipline, so be zealous and repent. It is a great act of love. And as Christians it is intended to help our brothers and sister to grow maturely in the Lord. To ignore his sin is to let him continue walking on the wrong path. Rebuking has a different effect on other people like this verse, Proverbs 9:8-9 Reprove a scorner, lest he hate thee: rebuke a wise man, and he will love thee. Give instruction to a wise man and he will be yet wiser: teach a just man and he will increase in learning. Another verse, Proverbs 12:1 Whoso loveth instruction loveth knowledge: but he that hateth reproof is brutish. But everything must be done with love and meekness and nuisance-free for God also does the convicting. John 16:7-9 Nevertheless I tell you the Truth; It is expedient for you that I go away: for if I go not away, the Comforter will not come unto you; but if I depart, I will send him unto you. And when he is come, he will reprove the world of sin, and of righteousness, and of judgment: Of sin, because they believe not on me;

CARNAL PASTORS MAKE A CARNAL CHURCH

C ARNAL PASTORS WILL eventually lead to Carnal Congregations. Since the pastor lives carnally, the deacons start to live like him too by engaging in small sins at first. It's a big domino effect or even a ripple effect. Soon the congregation no longer reads their Bible or takes God's Word seriously. Amy remembers when taking communion, she was no longer convicted to do so with sin in her heart. She noticed people nonchalantly took it out of tradition. When the Bible clearly says, "Wherefore whosoever shall eat this bread, and drink this cup of the Lord, unworthily, shall be guilty of the body and blood of the Lord." Leaders must set an example to follow otherwise the ripple effect will continue for generations to come. Even when there was a party a member invited most of the people in the church. In church they'd look so holy and modest but at the celebration they'd dress like the world, wearing tight, skimpy clothing, showing cleavage, short dresses and dance like it too. When there is no more remorse for our sin we become carnal and deaf to God's calling and lifestyle.

Amy remembers too how, when they prayed in church, the singing group moved around setting up mikes and chattering quietly causing distraction when the congregation was supposed to be talking to God. Some people were appalled at their disrespect towards God, our Creator. Other religions such as Catholicism, Buddhism, Judaism, etc. have great respect when someone is praying in church. Action like this became common because the priority was no longer Christ.

One day someone told Amy to forget about the whole situation since she was going to a different church now. This was after she told them that she was going to write a book about this pastor.

Her response to them was, "So you want me to let that pastor continue massaging young ladies and take them to places alone plus hurt people like you and me (hindering their spiritual growth)?" The person just remained speechless.

She then said, "Well, didn't he say he stopped massaging four years ago?"

"That's what he said at the meeting, but he never apologized to the congregation for his actions or to me." To Amy, this man had to be stopped because it was the right thing to do. Later on, she was compelled to write this poem.

<u>I WILL DO WHAT IS RIGHT</u>

I will do what is right, I will do what is right,
Though I stand alone and I'm the only woman.
Though they shout at me and call me names.
Though they throw me in a deep dungeon.
Though they feed me to the hungry lions.
Though they shackle me day and night.
Though they throw at me sticks and stones.
Though they mock me until my soul is torn.
I will do what is right for God alone.
For when I stand at His throne,
Will I be ashamed or stand strong?

MKG

A woman said to Amy, "You were an adult, so you should have known better than to go out to places with him. Why did you keep calling him? It's not like you were a child or helpless." Instead of blaming herself Amy decided to do research on the brain of a 20-year-old. Just because a person has reached 18 years of age it doesn't mean they can make an adult decision. Their brain, as a matter of fact, is still reorganizing itself, which then means that different thinking strategies are used as your brain becomes more like an adult brain. Child psychologists are being given a new directive which is that the age range they work with is increasing from 0-18 to 0-25. No matter what the intention was this pastor should have known better too. Instead of entertaining these young ladies he should have entertained his wife at home. Growing up we were taught to respect our pastors and elders. Amy was just doing what she was told. If her parents were close to her workplace she may have decided differently. She knew for sure she wouldn't ask for a ride to go to church.

A 30-plus-year church member who had been going to Pastor Janus's church ever since she was a wee little girl said to Amy, "Maybe the reason why he treated you like that is because he treats those closest to him more harshly than outside people." It was a pity that people thought like this. For the Bible says, Romans 12:10 — Be kindly affectioned one to another with brotherly love; in honour preferring one another. Luke 6:31 —And as ye would that man should do to you, Do ye also to them likewise. With God there is no prejudice of kin but love and longsuffering without boundary. By staying that long in that church she was left a baby Christian with no knowledge of God's Word and teachings. At times, people stayed there because of their friends and social life but by doing so they neglected and ignored their spiritual maturity.

Amy tried to tell one of her close friends what kind of pastor they had and all she could say was, "It's all by God's grace that he is a pastor." That friend of hers attended there for over 20 years. Someone else said, "Look at Saul and David; They committed sin when they were still kings, but God chose them." It was shocking how some people dismissed his outrageous acts. Amazingly, God brought these facts to Amy during one of her devotion times that when King Saul committed a sin according to the Bible God rejected him (I Samuel

16:1) and took away His Spirit from him (I Samuel 16:14). Plus, God departed and didn't answer him anymore neither through prophets or in dreams (I Samuel 28:15). As for David after he was anointed as a king, he did right in the beginning until he committed sin then when that happened God was displeased with him (2 Samuel 11:27c), sword shall never depart from David's house (2 Samuel 12:10a), God raised up evil against David (2 Samuel 12:13b), and the child who was born to David shall die (2 Samuel 12:14). Moreover, as for Solomon David's son he also lived right in the beginning and God gave him his desire, wisdom from God. But then later on he started marrying other women who had different gods and his heart turned from the Lord. In I King 11:9 God became angry with him and in verse 11 the Lord said he will rend the Kingdom from him and give it to someone else.

The sin we commit will not go unpunished. It doesn't matter if you're a king or a peasant, old or young, man or woman. God abhors sin and it is very important to Him that we genuinely confess our sin and live a holy life. This is when grace comes. No matter how much we sin He has a heart of forgiveness if we confess to our Redeemer. When we do not listen or obey to the voice of the Lord bad things will happen meaning He will punish us. He then reminded us to repent and in verses 23b and 24a of Chapter 12, He will teach us the good and the right ways. Only fear the Lord and serve him in Truth with all your heart. Tell me how is a pastor committing sin by living in the Truth? I Peter 1:15-16 But as he which hath called you is holy, so be ye holy in all manner of conversation; because it is written, Be ye Holy; for I am holy.

At the end, King David realized that without God our life will crumble and will become empty so before he died he reminded the next king how to live a righteous life, 1 Kings 2:3-4 And keep the charge of the LORD thy God, to walk in his ways, to keep his statutes, and his commandments, and his judgments, and his testimonies, as it is written in the law of Moses, that thou mayest prosper in all that thou doest, and whithersoever thou turnest thyself: That the LORD may continue his word which he spake concerning me, saying, If thy children take heed to their way, to walk before me in Truth with all their heart and with all their soul, there shall not fail thee (said he) a man on the throne of Israel.

In I King 14:16 and 15:26 and 15:34 there's a repeating phrase that said, "…and in his sin wherewith he made Israel to sin." Throughout generations when someone committed a sin whether great or small there was a ripple effect. We may not see it, but it does happen. Either you're a leader in a church, job, president of a country, etc. the decision that a leader makes can affect everyone. Will it make someone sin? Is our example causing a hindrance for someone to grow spiritually? Are we being a stumbling block to someone? So, it is important to do right.

Then one day, out of the blue, an unknown person texted Amy this message: Though we may be disheartened and stirred up this season and while it's painful having to go through fire, I recall these three things in this moment. He is with us in the fire. He won't allow it to be more than we can bear and 3rd...we will come out of it as gold shining for Him even more though the days get darker. Thank you Jesus for your faithfulness and working all these things for good and for your glory! Amen

It was the first encouragement Amy had ever received from another human being that put her feet slightly back on track. She hung on to every detailed Truth it had in it. Though she may never find out who this person is, God brought this text at a perfect time.

BE AWARE OF SPIRITUAL ABUSE

A LSO, BE AWARE of Spiritual Abuse from your pastors. Not many are aware of this or even know the term. Just like there are sexual abuses and physical abuses there is also Spiritual abuse. All this will result in psychological trauma and it can lead a person to depression, despair, despondency, and even suicide plus random anger, fear-motivated withdrawal, or to alleviating mechanisms like alcohol and medications. Here is an excerpt from Mike Fehlauer's book, *Exposing Spiritual Abuse*. While there are many spiritual abuses like an Atmosphere of Secrecy, An Elitist Attitude, one he speaks of that touched Amy's heart was the Power Positioning and Unquestioned Authority.

For Power Positioning Mike Fehlauer states, "There is certainly a place for biblical teaching on spiritual authority. But if a pastor preaches on this subject every Sunday, constantly reminding everyone that he is in charge, you can be sure that trouble is around the corner.

In an unhealthy church, the pastor actually begins to take the place of Jesus in people's lives. Commonly, people are told they cannot leave the church with God's blessing unless the pastor approves the decision. The implication is that unless they receive pastoral permission, not only will God not bless them, but they will also be cursed in some way, resulting in sure failure. Controlling spiritual leaders use this kind of reasoning to manipulate people.

We must understand the process a church goes through to reach this point of deception. Because many pastors measure their success through church attendance, they may become disappointed if people leave their church. If they are insecure, they may actually develop a doctrine in order to stop people from leaving. They may preach sermons about unconditional loyalty, using the biblical stories of David and Jonathan, or Elisha and Elijah.

By using examples like these, the leader can actually gain "biblical" grounds to control even the personal areas of his parishioners. A controlling leader may also attempt to instill a sense of obligation by reminding his congregation of everything he has done for them.

This kind of preaching causes church members to seek a position of favor with the pastor rather than a proper desire to "please God and not man." Jesus also condemned such man-pleasing when He told the Pharisees, "I have come in My Father's name, and you do not receive Me ... How can you believe, who receive honor from one another, and do not seek the honor that comes from the only God?" (John 5:43-44).

When we pursue the honor of men, we do so at the expense of our relationship with God. If we continue to do so, gradually men will take the place of God in our lives. An unhealthy soul tie is created, and our sense of confidence is determined by our standing with those in leadership. This kind of control will destroy people spiritually!

A healthy church will not allow genuine pastoral concern to cross the line into manipulation or control. A true shepherd will use his influence to draw church members into a close relationship with Jesus, who is the only "head of the church" (Eph. 5:23). A true shepherd realizes that the people in his congregation don't belong to him – they are God's flock."

For Unquestioned Authority he states, "In an unhealthy church, it is considered rebellion when someone questions decisions that are made or statements that are said from the pulpit. Granted, there are those who constantly question the leadership in any church – but often such constant questioning comes from an individual's critical attitude. Pastors must learn to deal with such questioning in a compassionate,

144 | Marissa Kline-Gonzales

positive manner. However, in an unhealthy church, any and all questions are considered threats to the pastor's "God-ordained" authority. Members who do dare to question their leaders or who do not follow their directives often are confronted with severe consequences.

A man from one church told me, "We were told that it is more important to obey leaders than to question what they are doing." He went on to say, "It was unthinkable to question the motives of the pastor."

For example, one couple, members of a church on the West Coast, decided to take a family vacation. This couple purchased their airline tickets and finalized the rest of their plans. They were looking forward to their long-needed time off. Once the pastor discovered their plans, he rebuked them for not getting his permission first and warned them not to go on the trip. They went anyway. Shortly after they returned, they were visited by some of the church's leadership. They were informed that by going on vacation against the pastor's wishes, they were in rebellion. To enforce the pastor's authority, there had to be some form of punishment applied. This couple was then informed that no one from the church was permitted to speak to them or have any contact with them for a time determined by the pastor. Even their children were not permitted to play with any of the other children from the church.

Pastors operating under a spirit of control are often convinced that they are the only ones who can accurately hear from God. Under the constant exposure to this spirit, members often become convinced that they indeed need their pastor to think for them. In essence, their personal fellowship with the Lord has been abdicated for a relationship with a man. As a result, they lose their confidence in being able to discern the will of God for their lives."

EVEN AFTER AMY left the church, she still heard inappropriate things that this same pastor was doing, such as, saying 'I love you' to a married woman instead of saying "I love you in Christ" or "The church loves you." Of course, this woman felt uncomfortable. She was going to church alone since her husband was not saved. She had hunger for God's Word and came faithfully whenever she wasn't working on Sunday. And just like Amy she loved the people and fellowshipping enriched her eagerness to come to church. When she asked other married ladies in the church if he did the same thing to them, they said no. Then a church member advised her to not tell anyone.

A young man in his mid-20s said to Amy that the pastor encouraged him to get a massage from a masseuse in the church. Amy knew this young man well and knew that he was still a very young Christian. He refused to get it for fear that once he did he might become addicted. Should a pastor be referring his church people to get a massage? This pastor's thinking definitely didn't align with God's Word.

Amy knew the Truth had to be told. She had this deep desire to express her feelings to the world and write down how she felt because she knew someone out there felt the same way. She wanted to warn people to watch out for this man! So, she posted this poem on her Facebook:

DO RIGHT

I'd rather have a pastor that does what is right.
Who sets an example from morning till night.
Who loves and fears God and will die for any man
Who walks what he preaches like helping the orphan.
'Cause if someone would ask me if my pastor does this,
I won't be ashamed to stand up and be proud of him.
To say good things and not tell a lie.
His reputation is important but what's that when you die?
Did I try to protect him by sweeping it under a rug?
No one will know it; many will just shrug.
I'll wait till it gets worse or hope it'll be forgotten.
You know how people are so busy and easy goin'.
When you protect someone that is doing something wrong
Or try to keep it a secret so no one will know,
You're not any better than the person next door.
Don't call yourself a Christian if you're not a salt of the world.

MKG

Even when Amy publicly announced this upcoming book on Facebook like she always did with her other books, showing the front and back cover, one of the leaders in that church accused her of having a vendetta towards the pastor. She said, "Our purpose in life is to share the gospel and bring people closer to our Lord. It seems like you only want to push people further away and hurt people, especially the pastor and his family. I don't know what your motive behind this is. This isn't being done in the spirit of love, grace or mercy. It's being done like you really hate the pastor and the church. Amy, you are hurting and going to hurt a lot of people."

Was Amy supposed to just turn a blind eye on this pastor's behavior? Was she just supposed to continue going to that church despite the many people that were being hurt? Was she supposed to just say, "Hey, my goal is to just share the gospel and nothing else?" Is that what the Bible tells us to do? No! God wants us to do the right thing like the many faithful saints mentioned in the scriptures. We are to help the hurt, stand-up against the wrong, encourage the weary and love the unloved. Truly, this leader's heart and mind were not solidly set in God's Word even though she herself attended Bible School. You cannot ignore potential spiritual abuse, especially when you are made aware it is happening. To be silent about the abuse makes you culpable in the abuse.

Amy's motives in her book have never changed to this day. She wants to help those who have also experienced an unhealthy church and encourage them to go back to church so that they may learn to love God again, trust God's people and read God's Word so that they can grow in peace, love and joy.

Amy knows that people inherently have sin natures and hide sin. A church should not hide sin but should preach against it. The Bible is against sin and condemns it. Jesus condemns sin but forgives us if we are repentant.

With God, she always remembers, nothing is impossible!

Over Ten Months Later

ON NEW YEAR'S Eve, while Amy Stiles drove home from work, she felt the thrill in the air. Families gathered together. Friends invited friends for the New Year celebration. The grocery stores were packed because people were buying food for the parties. She began to wonder what her family did last year during this special time. It was as if someone hit her in the stomach—it hit her like that. She was with her old church family celebrating the holiday. Then tears started to swell in her eyes and roll down her cheeks as she reminisced those days. It seemed like it was a long time ago when it was just last year.

Ten months had gone by and still no apology from the pastor. He was supposed to be her husband's godfather. They never invited them for family or church gatherings when they only lived five blocks away. Amy thought life was so unfair, that it was wrong they were the ones that had to leave the church instead of the pastor. She felt disappointed and betrayed. But she remained faithful in His Word, knowing that she would overcome this mountain.

After going to that church for 14 years she still couldn't believe what had happened. Twice she confronted him, twice he got upset, twice he accused her falsely and twice she was the one that apologized. Plus, he had the nerve to say, "I could have taken you to court."

With many anguished prayers and songs that God poured into her heart, Amy cried to Him—He was healing her, but it seemed to take so long. She still bled internally, so much so that the pain was almost too unbearable at times.

HERE ARE SOME Bible passages that talk about abstaining from taking a brother to court: 1 Corinthians 6:1-10 KJV—1 Dare any of you, having a matter against another, go to law before the unjust, and not before the saints? 2 Do ye not know that the saints shall judge the world? And if the world shall be judged by you, are ye unworthy to judge the smallest matters? 3 Know ye not that we shall judge angels? How much more things that pertain to this life? 4 If then ye have judgments of things pertaining to this life, set them to judge who are least esteemed in the church. 5 I speak to your shame. Is it so, that there is not a wise man among you? No, not one that shall be able to judge between his brethren? 6 But brother goeth to law with brother, and that before the unbelievers. 7 Now therefore there is utterly a fault among you, because ye go to law one with another. Why do ye not rather take wrong? Why do ye not rather [suffer yourselves to] be defrauded? 8 Nay, ye do wrong, and defraud, and that [your] brethren. 9 Know ye not that the unrighteous shall not inherit the kingdom of God? Be not deceived: neither fornicators, nor idolaters, nor adulterers, nor effeminate, nor abusers of themselves with mankind, 10 Nor thieves, nor covetous, nor drunkards, nor revilers, nor extortioners, shall inherit the kingdom of God.

The apostle Paul simply could not believe what these Corinthian Christians were doing. He told them that Christians should be able to handle their own matters instead of going to court, because when we get to heaven we will be the one judging the world and even the angels. Paul rebuked the man who had done the wrong. He spoke strongly to him, making him realize how serious his sin was. Paul said the only thing the man was 'gaining' was eternity with the unrighteous. The second reason why Christians should not take a brother to court is that it's possible the judge is not a Christian and to do so would allow the unbeliever to judge the believers. Christians are not to take or even threaten to take a brother to court. This just shows the immaturity of the pastor's spiritual being.

Pastor Janus would soon go on his 30th year Anniversary and Amy wondered how much more of his life was still unrevealed.

Amy asked herself each day of her Christian life if she had the fruit of the Spirit living in her, because if she couldn't change herself she couldn't preach and tell other people to change. The change must start within us. God must be seen in anything and everything that a person does and says and is. We are God's instruments and we must follow and live His way.

There could be many reasons why people leave the church, but Amy narrowed hers down to the several topics mentioned in this book. The main reason she wrote this book, though, was to hopefully help those who are in the same predicament she and her husband were in. Being broken from the people you trust and care about, and most of all, being mistreated by the person we all put our trust and respect in can be very difficult to overcome. Amy hoped and prayed that this book would help and encourage at least one person.

ALMOST A YEAR and a half after they left, Trinity United Church hosted a concert fundraiser to start an orphanage in the Philippines. It was such a contradiction that the church played a big part in this, knowing their pastor did these things. Think of the danger they put innocent children in. Amy was outraged. She was an orphan once and she pitied the children Pastor Janus would encounter. Didn't the church know what was right and wrong?

So, Amy asked a missionary what she thought of this situation. The missionary expressed disappointment, disagreed with the pastor's conduct, and advised her not to take part in the ministry.

One day, Amy's seven-year-old son randomly asked the pastor of her current church, "Who is in charge in this church?" My humble and patient pastor said, "God Jesus Christ." And Amy thought to herself, *That is a perfect answer.* She'd never heard anyone from her old church say that. Her new pastor never even paused to think but seemed to know the answer perfectly. She believed if a church is built on God, if a life is built on God and if one's happiness is built on God—then God will be glorified.

Amy recently read a book called, *When to Speak-Up and When to Shut-Up,* by Dr. Michael D. Sedler, a book that, in her opinion, every leader should read. The title may be a giveaway but there's more to the cover. Dr. Sedler gives a deep biblical insight of when to speak up and when to shut up, stating: "Because of a misuse of spoken words, destinies have been derailed, disunity has replaced unity, and nations have been destroyed. Our very lives, both physical and spiritual, depend upon our ability and willingness to speak out at the proper moment. And by the same token, silence can bring pain destruction and the inevitable onslaught of sin. Or it can allow the time for God's healing power to work in a life." Moreover, he states, "…Biblically, if we use silence as self-protection and as a way to avoid confrontation or hard decisions, we do not glorify God. *Psalm 115:17* says, *The dead do not praise the Lord, nor any who go down into silence.*" Our silence will only create a spiritual death within us." We must speak up for the Truth. As the saying goes, after all, evil will prosper when good men do nothing.

O N JANUARY 2018 Pastor Janus's wife called Amy's husband out of the blue. She said, "People that Amy has been talking to are coming up to us." She warned Amy that if she didn't stop talking to people they would file a case against her, sue her for defamation and get her fired from work. She said they have a recording of the meeting where Amy promised not to talk to people about the case. As far as Amy remembered, she didn't promise anything like that, so her statement was not true. The pastor's wife mentioned the people that had come up to them.

One was a family whose son went to the same karate class as her son. She remembered one of the family coming up to her, adamant to find out what happened between them and the pastor. Amy warned her, "If I tell you, you might end up going to a different church." She was okay with that and insisted that she know for her family's sake. So, Amy explained it all, from the pastor massaging and taking ladies out to the last word that Pastor Janus spoke, threatening a lawsuit and court hearing, which wasn't Christ-like. To this day, she still attends Amy's church and tells people that she came there because of Amy.

Another person she mentioned was a man. Amy saw him at a birthday party. Immediately they chatted together since they hadn't seen each other for a long time. He too wanted to know why they left. They were close to them remembering the days they went to the park and restaurants. A couple years ago, Amy spent time with his wife who just came from the Philippines. She helped her through the many adjustments. Amy at first said, "I'm not sure if you really want to know even though we left for a good reason." He was adamant. She never volunteered any information. These people knew her as a meek person and that she was not a trouble maker. So, they knew Amy and her family had to have left for a good reason but were puzzled about what it was. After she was done this man said, "And he's pastored you guys for how long?" She said 14 years, and emphasized how bold Pastor Janus was to threaten his own church family.

One day Amy picked up her son from school. She saw a familiar lady that used to go to the Filipino Church and decided to say Hi to her. The friendly greeting turned into a long talk. She said to Amy, "There used to be a lot of familiar faces in the church. Now many have left." After that she wanted to know why Amy's family left as well. Her eyes were opened, and she could not believe what she heard. She agreed that Pastor Janus should have apologized to the church for his actions. Now she was left with a decision to leave the church or stay.

Pastor Janus's wife also mentioned a pastor who came up to them but to Amy that could have been any of the pastors. Most of the pastors that she talked to disagreed with this pastor's behavior.

Most of the people that she talked to were all very adamant about wanting to know why they left. And so she thought the reason why they came to Pastor Janus and his wife was to verify and hear their side of the story. They heard her side and now they wanted to know his. There was nothing wrong with that. If people were adamant about wanting to know why they left, they should know. They had a right to know instead of learning about it so many years from now.

After their second threat, Amy decided to consult a lawyer. The lawyer asked her, "Do you guys work for the same company?" Her answer was no. The lawyer said, "There is no way Amy could lose her job. The job and church have no relation." Again, she knew it's a scare tactic. Also, he added, "It is not defamation if the story is true."

Truly, this pastor and his wife tried to run away from the Truth. Instead of apologizing and settling this in a peaceful way they'd rather hire a lawyer. God was definitely not pleased about this.

O N QUIET DAYS, Amy still looked at the paper she had from the ladies group she used to attend at her old church. These notes were written during her 14 years there. Many ladies wrote encouraging words about her:

You go out of your way to make people feel welcome and you are thoughtful. –Elizabeth

You are very sensitive in making people feel welcome and you are a gift to our church. –Sherine

Your ministry is encouragement especially to the quiet people at church. Keep on! You are also a good writer. –Eleanor

You are always available for anyone who needs encouragement. You love people and very hospitable. The visitors in the church are welcomed especially when you are there. –Ruth

You showed your faithfulness to God's Work in your unique way. Your friendship is very encouraging. You and Mark are lovely! –Mindy

Your quiet spirit and calm nature is completely opposite from mine, and I love how it reflects the Spirit of the Lord. Your heart for others in need and your willingness to help is always encouraging. Thank you for your gentle quiet spirit! –Molly

Your quiet ways speak volumes—no need for loudspeaker! Actions are better than words. Keep it up for Jesus. –Barbara

Your love for people and children are always an encouragement and blessing. The way you seek out people who are new to church or may not have a group and how you talk to them and make them feel welcome is a challenge and a blessing to me. –Angie

I appreciate your willingness to take care of newcomers. –Mandy

These words always encouraged Amy to remember that she would always have friends for life, like the song that goes, Friends are friends forever if the Lord is the

Lord of them. But where were they now? Sadly, only one stayed in touch with her. That is, when they felt like it. She had lots of memories of them in her mind, in pictures and even on videos but after she left they were just dust in the wind. Most of them didn't send her family Christmas cards anymore or come to her house or even call to say Hi. Now there was a big gap in her life that was sometimes best left forgotten or ignored. Nevertheless, Amy always found comfort in God's Word and through this she was able to write this poem.

NOT THROUGH THE STORM YET

Now I'm sleeping better, though not through yet from
the storm,
There is still lightning splashing somewhere but
thunder has calmed down more.
My prayer is heard after all, my voice tells it all.
I can't handle my own problems; to the Creator I fall.
I know my weaknesses, my sometimes faithless heart.
Carrying that entire burden is tearing me apart.
I know He is here waiting for me to come.
He wants me close by His side, no matter how much
ton.
The wind and seas obey him; everything turns calm.
I want my life to be peaceful again, one day at a time.

MKG

To this day, the two-faced pastor still preaches at the same church in the same city and continues to raise funds for his overseas orphanage and Medical Mission Ministry. He might just be down the street from your home. Be very aware where your money is going. If you think something is not right, it usually is not.

<u>Advice on Overcoming an Unhealthy Church</u>

KEEP A JOURNAL. Journals are a great way to say and write down everything you feel. Amy Stiles wrote so much that it became a book. Through many songs that God placed in her heart and the solitary nature of writing poems, He gave Amy healing and peace that only comes from Him. While the world may turn to drinking, drug abuse and smoking, a child of God must hang on to God's Word. God is faithful to those who are faithful to Him.

FIND A NEW CHURCH. Everyone knows that church contains something we all need. If ever we abandon a church for a time we will realize that we are the one that suffers. We end up blaming God for everything.

Don't give up hope on church. Remain faithful by looking for a church for the sake of your family and for you. Hebrew 10:25 says, "Not forsaking the assembling of ourselves, as the manner of some is, and so much the more, as ye see the day approaching."

TALK TO CHRISTIAN MENTORS. After Amy left her church, she talked to many mature Christians (i.e. Bible professors, pastors, Christian radio station hosts, and Bible teachers), regarding her situation. Proverbs 11:14 says, "Where no counsel is, the people fall: but in the multitude of counselors there is safety." Many of the people Amy spoke with had agreed with her decision to leave the church. It is imperative that you surround yourself with people who have the same beliefs and morals.

KEEP PRAYING. I Thessalonians 5:17 says, "Pray without ceasing." There is power in prayer and though we may not know the plan that God has in store for us we must keep on praying to keep us positive and sane.

MAKE NEW FRIENDS. You must go on. Your friends may still be at that church and may not know what happened to you. If they are your true friends, they will call and keep in touch. Amy thanks the Lord that she stayed friends with many old friends from that church. Although, she also thanks God for the new friends He brought into her life.

As Christians, we must remember that everything happens for a reason. Both good and bad is all part of God's plan to mold us in the way God wants us to grow. Most of all, God doesn't make things happen from only good experiences; He often changes bad, traumatic or overwhelming challenges into the good situation, making us into mature, strong Christians.

For example, think of the lives of Job, Joseph, Moses, Sampson, and so many others. God either blessed them, answered their prayers and/or gave them the desires of their hearts.

Remember when there is a trial that there is triumph and where there is a test there is a testimony. Through this experience, Amy was able to see God's Almighty hands working in her life. She saw that she was a person who loved God by trying to do what was right despite all the opposition she faced. She was a person who feared God rather than man. For in the end God will be our judge.

References

The Bible. KJV, NIV

Fehlauer, Mike. *Exposing Spiritual Abuse*. Creation House, 2001.

Towns, Dr. Elmer. *Ordination*.

Sedler, Dr. Michael, D. *When to Speak-Up and When to Shut-Up*. Revell, 2006.

McWhirter, Jake. *Article*.

Arterburn, Steve. *More Jesus, Less Religion*. WaterBrook Press, 2000.

Gentle, Derek. *A Study in the Biblical Role of Deacons*. http://www.baptiststart.com/print/role_of_deacons.html

Hullinger, Dr. Jerry. *Exposition*.

Pulpit. *Commentary*.

Daman, Glenn. *When Sheep Squabble-Dealing with Conflict in the Smaller Church*. http://enrichmentjournal.ag.org/200502/200502_086_squabble.cfm

Specht, Charles. *Twenty Qualification Every Pastor Must Possess*. http://www.charlesspecht.com/20-qualifications-every-pastor-must-possess/

Sanford, David. *Overcoming a Bad Church Experience*. Focus On The Family.
https://www.focusonthefamily.com/marriage/growing-together-spiritually/spiritual-intimacy/overcoming-a-bad-church-experience.

Henry, Matthew. *Commentaries.*

Barnes, Albert. *Commentary.*

Bibletools.org.

Wikipedia.org.

Author Biography

AFTER GRADUATING FROM high school, Marissa Kline‑Gonzales attended Word of Life Bible Institute (1999). She wrote her first book *Orphaned, Fostered and Adopted,* a biography about her life, in 2009. She has been a flight attendant for over 15 years, married for over 10 years and has two children. She recently published her *Collections of 89 Poems* in 2016. Collect all the volumes!

Made in the USA
Middletown, DE
16 September 2019